W28

WILD SECRET

TYSON WILD BOOK TWENTY EIGHT

TRIPP ELLIS

D1316696

Copyright © 2021 by Tripp Ellis

All rights reserved. Worldwide.

This book is a work of fiction. The names, characters, places, and incidents, except for incidental references to public figures, products, or services, are fictitious. Any resemblance to persons, living or dead, actual events, locales, or organizations is entirely coincidental, and not intended to refer to any living person or to disparage any company's products or services. All characters engaging in sexual activity are above the age of consent.

No part of this text may be reproduced, transmitted, downloaded, decompiled, uploaded, or stored in or introduced into any information storage and retrieval system, in any form or by any means, whether electronic or mechanical, now known or hereafter devised, without the express written permission of the publisher except for the use of brief quotations in a book review.

WELCOME

Want more books like this?

You'll probably never hear about my new releases unless you join my newsletter.

SIGN UP HERE

1

——

J D's eyes lit up. "There's something down there."

He stared at his phone's display, excitement building on his face.

"What is it?" I asked.

"I don't know, but it's something." He had a sly grin.

The *Avventura* swayed gently on the swells. The brilliant sun hung high in the royal blue sky, glimmering across the teal water.

It was a perfect afternoon.

We had spent the better part of the day fishing and *treasure hunting*. I use the term loosely.

JD had programmed the sonar drone to search a pre-determined grid. The device relayed a 3-D image back to his cell phone. The state-of-the-art gadget was next-level technology. I'm not sure how much he paid for the damn thing, and I didn't want to ask.

We had found quite a few things on the seafloor in the course of our adventures, but never the elusive treasure of Jacques De La Fontaine.

It didn't matter. The journey was half the fun.

We lounged on the aft deck of the superyacht, fishing poles in hand, JD wearing his traditional Hawaiian shirt and cargo shorts. His long blond hair fluttered with the breeze. With his new discovery, he was up and out of his seat. "I say we go down and take a look."

I surveyed the screen. "I don't think that's what we're looking for."

It was just a small shape and certainly not the pattern of a sunken Spanish Galleon or pirate ship.

It was likely all that remained of the old ships were the cannons and the precious coins strewn about the seafloor. Everything else had rotted away—several hundred years of the ocean doing its magic to reclaim the fabled ships.

JD darted inside to grab the gear. Once he got his mind set on something there was no stopping him.

What the hell—it was worth taking a look.

I followed him into the salon and grabbed the scuba equipment. We had prepped the tanks before we set out for the day.

We recovered the drone. JD hosed it down and toweled it off. It looked like a Tomahawk missile with a propeller.

We did last-minute safety checks, donned our gear, raised the diver down flag, and plunged into the water from the swim platform.

It was an easy dive. It wasn't that deep in this particular location. I nosed down and finned toward the bottom, JD beside me.

The water was almost 80 degrees. The dull rumble of the ocean filled my ears. Bubbles roiled toward the surface, and rays of sunlight penetrated the water. The silhouette of the superyacht floated above as we plunged deeper.

A recent storm had blown through the area and had stirred up the seafloor. You never knew what a storm might uncover that had been hidden for centuries.

I was skeptical about what we'd find, but I'd be lying if I said I wasn't a little bit thrilled at the possibility of discovering Spanish gold stolen by the infamous French pirate.

As we plunged deeper, it became clear this was not the gravesite of a Spanish Galleon or pirate ship. There was no clump of gold medallions buried in the soft sand.

Instead, the edge of a steel drum protruded from the sandy bottom. It looked like it had been there for quite some time —rusted and corroded.

I could see the disappointment on JD's face through his mask.

He shook his head and pointed to the surface.

We were down here already. I figured we might as well investigate further. All kinds of things end up at the bottom of the ocean. Things fall off shipping vessels all the time. People dump things they shouldn't.

I began scooping the sand away from the barrel, trying to reveal more of it. JD joined in, and clouds of sediment swirled around, creating a milky haze.

It didn't take long to reveal the *toxic chemical* sticker on the side of the barrel. It was barely legible at this point.

We uncovered about two-thirds of the barrel. It looked intact and still sealed. Together we tried to shift the barrel in the sand, but the damn thing was heavy.

We left it and decided to return to the surface. We broke through the water and climbed onto the swim platform. I spat the regulator from my mouth and took off my mask. I slipped the tank from my shoulders.

"What do you think?" JD asked.

"I say we call the Department of Environmental Protection and let them deal with it. Could be seeping toxic chemicals into the water."

I stood up, water dripping from my body, and lugged the tank up to the aft deck. I toweled off and made a few phone calls. I got transferred to several different departments. I sat on hold for 30 minutes, then finally talked to someone in the Office of Emergency Response. I spoke with a delightful young woman and told her about the situation.

I don't think she listened to a word I said. In her defense, we were pretty far out, and the cell signal dropped occasionally.

"If you go to our website, you can see a list of independent contractors for removal," she said. "Be aware that you will be responsible for all fees, and any potential fines."

"I'm sorry, maybe I wasn't clear. I am a deputy with the Coconut County Sheriff's Department. We discovered a potential environmental hazard. This isn't my barrel, and it didn't fall off my boat."

"Doesn't the county have a dive team that can remove the barrel?"

"Hazardous waste disposal isn't our area," I said.

She huffed. "Where is the location of this barrel?"

I gave her the coordinates.

"Okay, I'll have our department deal with it."

"How long will that take?"

"I don't know. It depends on how backlogged they are."

I gave her my number and asked her to follow up with me. I doubted I would ever hear from her again, but I planned on pestering them until the toxic barrel was removed.

The afternoon had evaporated, and we needed to get back to Coconut Key. There was an event we couldn't miss. We weighed anchor and JD manned the helm, cruising us back to the island.

"To one more shift," Chuck said with a smile, raising his glass.

We all clinked glasses, cheered, and sipped the whiskey. Half the department was in *Flanagan's* for Chuck's retirement party. It was probably the ideal time to commit a crime—somewhere else.

Erickson, Faulkner, Mendoza, Robinson, and Sheriff Daniels were all there. So were Denise and Brenda, the medical examiner. It was Denise's day off, and the luscious red-head pranced around in shorts and a tight tank top— always a pleasant sight.

Chuck was in his mid-60s and had spent the past 30 years on the force. He was a good cop and a likable guy. He had a round face and a rounder belly. His dark hair was peppered with more gray than he'd like, and his bad knees from old football injuries were catching up with him.

It was time.

He'd written enough tickets and chased down enough bad guys. He'd been in a patrol unit almost the entire time. He'd been shot twice and gotten lucky both times. Still, he liked being out on the street and interacting with people. Somehow, after 30 years in a patrol car, seeing the worst that people had to offer, he still had faith in humanity—not something every cop could say.

Flanagan's was your typical Irish pub and a favorite among deputies. It had that old-school vibe—dark mahogany woodwork, paneled walls on one side of the establishment, exposed brick on the other. There were plenty of cozy booths, and black and white pictures hung on the walls.

The venue was narrow, like a shotgun shack—booths and tables upfront, the bar in the middle, and the restrooms and an office area in the back. There was a quarter pool table and a dartboard. The drinks were cheap, and the bartender, Rick, had a heavy hand. There was a good variety of beer and ale. The jukebox played mostly old-school rock 'n' roll. This wasn't the kind of place where you'd hear candy-coated pop rock or droning EDM music. Rick knew everyone's name and what they drank—well, the regulars, at least.

For some reason, the bar had been growing in popularity among the younger crowd. It had suddenly become hip and trendy. It was probably a fad that would last for a few months before the crowd moved on to the next cool place. A lot of people would come in and pregame at Flanagan's because of the cheap drinks before hitting the more expensive bars on the strip. A block off of Oyster Avenue, Flanagan's was close to the action but didn't get as many tourists.

"So what the hell are you gonna do with yourself now?" JD asked.

"Besides drive Ellie crazy? I'm not sure." He paused. "I know what I *want* to do."

"What's that?" I asked.

"You're gonna think I'm crazy," Chuck said.

"We already think that," JD snarked.

"I've got my eye on a piece of property in Montana—300 acres of riverfront property. Got a nice little ranch house and a stable for horses. I figure I'd raise some cattle, hunt, fish, and enjoy the rugged outdoors."

"How does Ellie feel about that?" I asked.

"She's not sold on the concept."

"You realize they have actual winters up there," JD said. "And there's no ocean."

"I've been in Coconut Key for the majority of my life. I think it's time for a change. Plus, if I stay here, I don't think I'll be able to let the *job* go. I'll be trying to pull over people on a daily basis. I love this place, don't get me wrong, but I know too much about the shady side."

"Every place has a shady side," JD said.

"Yeah, but maybe if I go somewhere else, I could pretend it doesn't exist." He sighed and frowned. "Which reminds me, I need to talk to you boys about something," he said.

We were all ears.

"Not here. Let's save it for later. No shop talk tonight."

We smiled and clinked glasses again.

A scowl twisted Chuck's face as a drunk guy stumbled by

with his girlfriend. He was probably 21. He had a thin build with blond hair and blue eyes, which were glassy and bloodshot.

His blonde girlfriend was smoking hot—tanned skin, shorts, tight bikini top.

The guy caught sight of Chuck and smiled. "Don't worry, Deputy Atwood. I'm not driving."

He lifted his glass, sipped his drink, and staggered away with the hot blonde.

"Friend of yours?" JD asked.

"That's Nick Hartsell's kid, Cameron. Popped him for DUI not long ago. His dad worked some kind of deal, paid the fine, and the kid got off scot-free."

"By the looks of things, it won't be long till he gets arrested again," JD said.

"I guess that's not really my problem anymore," Chuck said. "I'll leave it up to you guys to carry the torch of justice."

"You're gonna miss this," JD said.

"I know. But I ain't gonna miss it *that* much."

We laughed and ordered another round. Chuck wasn't paying for a thing tonight.

Cameron staggered out with his girlfriend and ambled down the sidewalk, heading toward Oyster Avenue.

A few minutes later, two guys burst in wearing ski masks, wielding shotguns. One of them racked a black sawed-off with a pistol grip and shouted, "If you haven't figured it out, this is a robbery. Do as you're told, and nobody gets hurt. Now is not the time to be a hero."

These guys were, perhaps, the dumbest criminals on the island. Robbing a cop bar was certainly up there on the list of stupid things to do. Clearly, they hadn't done their homework. Half the people in *Flanagan's* were packing.

"My friend is gonna go around with a bag," Mr. Shotgun said. "Throw in your wallet, jewelry, and cell phones."

The thug's accomplice moved around, holding a black duffel bag as patrons began to toss in their valuables.

"Boys, you're making a big mistake," Sheriff Daniels said. "Now, how about you put the weapon down and surrender before this thing gets out of hand."

The thug swung the shotgun toward the sheriff, the big angry barrel staring him down. "Shut the hell up! Do as you're told!"

Daniels sighed. "You realize you're standing amid half the department. Some in uniform, some in plainclothes."

The thug's wide eyes glanced around, fully realizing the gravity of the situation. In their haste to knock off the joint, they hadn't really noticed who occupied the bar. But it was slowly sinking in.

The thug swallowed hard but stood firm.

3

You could almost smell the fear oozing from the thug. Sweat soaked his armpits. His wide eyes beamed through his ski mask.

Denise happened to be standing behind him. He had disregarded her as a threat.

Big mistake.

Never underestimate a red-head.

Denise snatched a subcompact that was holstered in her waistband and aimed it at *Mr. Shotgun*.

He never saw it coming.

"Drop the weapon, now!" she shouted in a voice that was not to be trifled with. "Or you're going to have a really big hole in your head."

The thug tightened.

The air was tense.

The *Bag Boy* caught sight of the situation, dropped the duffel bag, pulled a gun from his waistband, and aimed it at Denise.

My heart leaped into my throat. The situation had the potential to go downhill quickly.

It all happened in slow motion.

My hand had been resting on the grip of my pistol, holstered in my waistband, waiting for the right time.

Now was just about that time.

Within a fraction of a second, every deputy had their weapon drawn and aimed at one of the two scumbags.

"It would be a good idea for you guys to give yourselves up," Daniels said.

After a moment's hesitation, Mr. Shotgun raised his hands in the air.

Mendoza snatched the shotgun from his grasp. "On the ground, now!"

The thug's accomplice held his silver semi-automatic pistol aimed at Denise. His hand trembled slightly, and his wide eyes flicked about, glancing at all the armed deputies and the barrels of their pistols.

He hesitated a moment, then sprinted toward the door.

Mendoza pounced on Mr. Shotgun and slapped the cuffs around his wrists.

Bag Boy pushed through the door and took off running down the sidewalk.

With Denise out of harm's way, the lump in my throat vanished. I gave chase, racing across the bar, sprinting out the door.

Bag Boy's sneakers slapped against the sidewalk as he sprinted toward the corner.

My legs drove me forward, and my heart pounded as I chased after him. Pedestrians shrieked and parted as the masked thug barreled past them.

He turned at the intersection, hauling ass down a narrow one-way lane that ran behind the bars.

I rounded the corner, chasing after the scumbag.

We raced down the narrow passage past dumpsters and the back end of all the establishments that faced Oyster Avenue. It was a long stretch with nowhere else to go. There were a few mopeds parked out back and bikes chained to racks.

The thug made a hard left at the next block and continued down the cobblestone sidewalk that was lined with palm trees. He crossed Oyster, darted past a few cafés, then cut across the street onto Fitzsimmons Drive.

There were more cobblestone sidewalks and antique lamp posts. He ran past more shops and street vendors, scurried across the street at the next intersection, and barreled north on Florence Street.

My chest heaved for breath as we shot past more storefronts and wide-eyed tourists. A burly dude with his girlfriend stuck out his leg and tripped the thug.

He ate the pavement, and his silver pistol skidded into the street. By the time he sprang to his feet, I tackled him back to the ground, crushing his ribs against the concrete.

He groaned as the air rushed from his lungs.

"Game's over, scumbag!" I grabbed his wrist and wrenched his arm behind his back. I slapped the cuffs on without much trouble. Then I yanked the dipshit to his feet.

I thanked the tourist.

"Anytime."

I told him to stop by the station and get a commendation from the department—a little souvenir to bring home. He seemed excited about the proposition.

I read the dirt-ball his rights and dragged him back to *Flanagan's*. It was a long walk and went by much slower than the initial chase. We both heaved for breath. I yanked the mask off his head. "You didn't think too much about what you were doing, did you?"

He glared at me.

"Are you new in town? Did you not know where you were walking into?"

"I ain't saying shit to you."

"You're lucky no one got hurt," I said. "The last thing you want to do is kill a cop."

4

We took the perps back to the station and filled out after-action reports. Chuck certainly wouldn't miss those in retirement.

After we wrapped up, we hit *Tide Pool* to blow off a little steam. The energy from Chuck's retirement party had long since dissipated. He called it an early evening and went home.

JD and I sat with Denise at a patio table by the outside pool, watching scantily-clad beauties frolic. The smell of piña coladas and strawberry daiquiris drifted through the air. Girls splashed and giggled, their soaking wet bikinis clinging to sumptuous mounds, the fabric almost transparent.

"You're pretty quick with that pistol," I said to Denise. "Is that the one I got you for Christmas?"

She grinned, and her emerald eyes sparkled. "It sure is. And just because I sit behind a desk all day doesn't mean I don't know how to use it."

"You could have gotten yourself killed," I said.

She frowned at me. "What was I supposed to do? Sit there and do nothing?"

I shrugged. "It's a good thing his buddy didn't start squeezing off rounds at you."

She made a pouty face. "Aw, is someone concerned?"

"I'm just looking out for my fellow deputy."

She rolled her eyes. "If anyone needs to exercise caution, it's you two."

"Don't look at me," JD said. "He's the wildcard. Not me."

She scoffed, knowing better. "You're both wildcards."

A guilty smirk curled on Jack's lips. "No risk, no reward."

"Well, I took a risk, and it paid off."

Jack lifted his glass, and we toasted.

We sipped our drinks and took in the atmosphere.

"Are you guys going to the fundraiser?" Denise asked.

"Hadn't given it a whole lot of thought," JD said.

"It's black tie at the *Seven Seas*. Free drinks," she said in singsong.

Jack perked up. "Well, in that case, I might have to consider it."

"Stella Turner puts it on every year. I figure it's a good excuse to get all dolled up. I could use a chaperone or two."

Any excuse to see Denise in evening wear was a good thing. She cleaned up well. *I imagined she dirtied up well too.*

"I believe we can provide you a security escort," I said.

She chuckled. "I'm sure you can."

"What charity is this benefiting again?" JD asked.

"It's that Coconut Key Forward Fund that the state attorney is involved with. They give grants to youth organizations, rehabilitation programs, that kind of thing. Community building."

"Get potential donors liquored up on the free drinks and have them open their checkbooks," JD said.

"Something like that."

"I'll be sure to leave my checkbook at home."

Denise scowled at him playfully. "Don't be a miser. You can give back to the community."

JD's face crinkled. "I give back to the community. I don't take a salary to do this job, and we put our lives on the line every day."

Denise rolled her eyes. "If you guys didn't do this, you'd invent new ways to skirt death on a daily basis."

JD and I exchanged a sheepish glance. There was no argument there. We were both adrenaline junkies. The job fulfilled that need and had the added bonus of actually doing some good.

"When is it again?" I asked.

"Saturday night. 7 PM."

"It's a date," I said with a grin.

The sultry redhead gave me a suspicious glance. "I wouldn't go that far."

"Can I get you guys another round?" a waitress asked as she sauntered by.

It didn't take much persuasion.

"One more, then I turn into a pumpkin," Denise said. "I gotta work tomorrow, and some of us actually need this job."

The waitress returned a moment later with our drinks, and JD picked up the tab. We nursed the drinks for a while, then JD and I escorted Denise back to her banana yellow SUV.

Lights from the bars and restaurants bathed the street. Tipsy tourists wandered up and down the strip. Palm trees lined the avenue, and the smell of pizza and fajitas from street vendors wafted about. Music from live bands spilled onto the street. There was an average crowd for a weekday, but not the madhouse of the weekends.

We found Denise's SUV parked on a side street. She gave us both a hug, and the sweet scent of her perfume filled my nostrils. She was definitely a good hugger.

"You boys behave," she said before hopping into the SUV.

"Not a chance," JD replied.

We watched her pull away, then walked down the block toward Jack's Porsche. He took a deep, contemplative breath. "You know, Chuck's retirement has got me thinking..."

"You're not thinking about hanging this up, are you? You're not *that* old," I teased.

He gave me a friendly scowl. "No. I'm thinking you should retire before the fundraiser. Then you're free and clear to let the magic happen. I see the way you two look at each other. There's a palpable energy in the air when you two are in the same room together. Life is short. Screw departmental policy. You need to make it happen."

"She doesn't want a guy like me."

"Oh, yes, she does."

I shook my head. "No, she doesn't. You see what happens to the people that are close to me. There are people out there that want me dead. Elias Fink by way of Sophia Breslin."

"Denise is a big girl. She can take care of herself. She proved that today."

"Not taking the risk."

"How about you let her make that decision? What are you going to do? Keep everybody at arm's-length the rest of your life? Push away the people that care about you the most?

"If it keeps them alive, yes."

"You do a damn good job of it. Or maybe you're just afraid to commit?"

I laughed. "You're one to talk."

Jack shrugged innocently. "I've committed six times."

"If you *committed* six times, then you didn't really commit, did you?"

His face crinkled. "Don't twist this around on me. We're psychoanalyzing you."

I laughed. "No we're not."

We hopped into the Miami Blue convertible 911 Turbo. JD cranked up the engine, and classic rock blasted from the speakers. He put the car in gear and pulled away from the curb. The night air swirled around the cabin, blowing his blond hair as we cruised across the island to the marina at *Diver Down*.

I thought about what he said. It brought up a complicated range of emotions. My past was out there stalking me. It would likely haunt me forever. At any moment, an assassin's bullet could find me. And it wasn't just Elias Fink or Sophia Breslin I had to worry about. There were plenty of bad actors out there that wanted to see me six feet under. And that list grew on a regular basis. It wasn't just ghosts from my clandestine past. Every scumbag we put away created another person with a vendetta. I'd never be able to stop looking over my shoulder.

Maybe Chuck had the right idea—move to a secluded piece of property, settle in, live a simple, anonymous life. Of course, I'd have to start with a new identity and stay off the radar. I was no stranger to becoming invisible. I wouldn't even tell Isabella, my handler at *Cobra Company*.

It was food for thought.

A thought that lasted half a second. Hiding out just wasn't my style.

Eliminate all the bad guys... that seemed like a better option.

JD turned into the parking lot at *Diver Down* and pulled around to the dock. There was a little activity within the restaurant and bar.

I hopped out of the car and told him I'd catch up with him in the morning. He pulled away, and the engine howled as he disappeared into the night.

I ambled down the dock to the *Avventura*. Boats swayed in their slips, and the moon cast a pale glow over the marina. The calming sound of waves lapping against fiberglass hulls drifted through the air.

I crossed the passerelle to the aft deck of the superyacht and slid open the sliding glass door to the salon. I was greeted by an excited Jack Russell Terrier. Buddy bounced and barked. I knelt down and petted him and scratched his chin. I grabbed his leash and took him out for a walk before bed, then settled in for the evening.

Daniels called bright and early the next morning. Amber rays of sunlight blasted into my stateroom. I snatched the phone from the nightstand and swiped the screen. The sheriff's gruff voice filtered through the speaker, "Did you nitwits find some type of toxic waste in the ocean?"

"Yeah, what's going on?" I said in a scratchy, dry voice.

"I got a call from DEP. They sent a salvage crew to recover that barrel."

"They got on that fast."

"It seems they take that kind of thing seriously. Anyway, it contained a little more than toxic material. It's sitting in a warehouse at a containment facility. I need you and numb-nuts to get over there right now."

5

DEP had contracted with *KNG Salvage*. Among other things, they were a licensed hazmat removal and disposal operation. Fully bonded and insured and permitted with the state. They dealt mostly with boats that sank and had the potential to leak fuel and oil into the water. They weren't the company to call if you had an oil tanker with a massive spill. But they were more than capable of pulling a steel drum out of the water and making sure its hazardous contents got disposed of in a way that didn't damage the environment.

The medical examiner's van was in the parking lot when we arrived. We parked the car, hopped out, and after a quick stop in the main office, we were directed to the scene. An employee named Thad escorted us toward a steel warehouse not far from the dock where a salvage tug was moored. The whole compound was surrounded by a chain-link fence topped with razor wire.

Thad was in his early 20s. He had a slender build and dark hair. His eyes were wide with excitement. "I've been working here a few years, and we've pulled a lot of things out of the ocean, but never anything like this."

Gulls squawked in the sky, floating on the draft. The sun glimmered on the water. Deckhands hustled about the salvage tug.

We walked through the open bay door of the warehouse. The flash of a camera bounced off the walls as a forensic photographer snapped photos of the contents of the barrel. He wore an industrial respirator and a white PPE suit. So did Brenda as she hovered over the container, peering inside.

"What have you got?" I asked as we approached.

The stench emanating from the barrel twisted my nose, and I quickly realized why they were wearing respirators.

"See for yourself," Brenda said, her muffled voice filtering through the mask.

I held my breath, stepped close, and leaned over the barrel.

My face soured.

I stepped away and filled my lungs with a breath of fresh air when I was in the clear.

JD gave a gander as well. Curiosity had gotten the best of him. He didn't linger long and joined me a few feet away from the barrel.

Crammed into the sludge-filled container was a skeleton.

Surrounded by black goo, the flesh had completely decomposed. The remains looked like something out of a horror movie. It was the kind of barrel that was never supposed to be opened. The kind of container that could start the zombie apocalypse. I halfway expected the gooey skeleton to climb out of the barrel and start gnawing on flesh.

Brenda pulled off her mask and joined us. "You guys find the strangest things."

"Tell me about it," I replied.

"She's been in there for some time."

"She?"

Brenda nodded. "Hard to say how long. Looks like there's a serial number stenciled on the barrel. I'll see if I can track down its origin. The warning label says it contains sodium hydroxide—a common chemical used in industrial settings. It would have dissolved the flesh rapidly, leaving the skeleton mostly intact. I'm going to go out on a limb and say she didn't get in that barrel all by herself."

"Somebody killed her, stuffed her in a barrel full of chemicals, and dumped her at sea," JD muttered. "They almost got away with it."

"You haven't caught them yet," Brenda snarked.

"It's early. Give it time." Jack smiled.

A slight chuckle escaped her lips. "I'll let you know what I find out."

We left the warehouse and walked back to the parking lot.

Paris Delany arrived with a news crew. They hopped out of the van, and the cameraman shouldered his rig and started filming. The sound guy ran behind the gorgeous blonde as she approached.

I stifled a groan.

"Deputy Wild, what can you tell us about the situation?"

"No comment," I said, following JD's previous advice.

"Is it true a body was discovered in a barrel?"

The camera focused in tight on me.

I climbed into the passenger seat of the Porsche, and JD cranked up the engine. I smiled and waved as we pulled out of the parking lot and headed back to the station.

Brenda had a lot of work to do. The chemical needed to be positively identified. Then the barrel needed to be moved to the medical examiner's office, the remains extracted and analyzed, then the waste disposed of.

After we filled out paperwork, I found Denise at her desk. Her perfectly manicured fingers clacked the keyboard. Phones rang, and the daily hustle of activity filled the air. Rays of sunlight filtered in through the blinds, and motes of dust swirled in the shafts. Deputies fielded complaints and processed perps.

JD grabbed a cup of coffee and brought one for me loaded up with cream and sugar. It was early, and the coffee relatively fresh.

"I heard about your discovery," Denise said. "That's really creepy."

I agreed.

"How horrible. I couldn't imagine that. Do you think the girl was alive when she got stuffed into the barrel?"

"For her sake, I hope not."

"I'll never understand why people do the things they do."

"Search the records for missing females over the last couple of years."

"Could you be more specific?"

"Not yet. Keep it broad. I just want to get a head start on this thing."

"Will do."

Jack's daughter called from Los Angeles. Scarlett shrieked into the phone. "Have you seen it?"

"Seen what?"

6

"The trailer for the Bree Taylor project is out!" Scarlett squealed. "I'm sending you a link. Watch it and call me back."

She hung up the phone, and a moment later, the text buzzed through. I clicked the link, and it took me to the clip. The logo for the studio flashed on the screen, and the trailer began.

I called JD over, and he huddled beside me, his eyes glued to the screen.

Scarlett had been cast as the lead in the film. It was based on the last three days of Bree Taylor's life. Three days that I was in the middle of.

At the time of her death, Bree was topping the box office charts. She had it—the elusive quality that every aspiring actor desires. She was a classic movie star in every sense of the word. She had all the beauty and glamour of old-school Hollywood. Ironically, her death cemented her as an icon that would be remembered for generations.

Scarlett filled her shoes well.

They couldn't have cast a better actress in the role.

Scarlett was breathtaking when she appeared on screen, and her likeness to Bree was stunning. Her hair and makeup were done to perfection, and the features of her face were contoured to look more like Bree.

I had been on set during several days of filming and watched on the video monitors. Her resemblance sent chills up my spine at the time. Now, watching the final product, it was even more remarkable. She had studied Bree's mannerisms and embodied the star perfectly. Every nuance, every smirk, every flick of the hair and bat of the eyelashes.

She *was* Bree.

The trailer ended, and the title flashed on the screen. The studio had kicked around a number of titles—*Death on the Riviera, The Last Icon, Fatal Blonde.*

They finally settled simply on *Bree.*

It appeared on screen in a beautiful script font—carefree, almost whimsical.

JD beamed with pride at his daughter's accomplishment. "That kid is going places."

If the movie was half as good as the trailer, it would be a hit. I had sold the story to the studio and was due a nice chunk of residuals on the backend. But more than that, I wanted Scarlett to achieve success. This was a pivotal moment in her career.

I called Scarlett back right away and congratulated her. I put the call on speakerphone. "I'm here with Jack. We just watched the trailer. It was amazing. You look fantastic."

"I'm so excited!"

"You're making your old man proud," JD said.

"You guys are coming for the premiere, right?"

"We wouldn't miss it."

"The press tour is starting up. Things are gonna get really crazy."

"Just don't let it all go to your head," JD said.

"I won't. But I can enjoy this moment."

"As you should."

"Gotta run," she said. "Love you guys. Oh, by the way, I have something to tell you when you get out here. Show you, really."

JD groaned. "Should I be concerned?"

She laughed. "You'll see."

The call was over as quickly as it began.

JD's enthusiasm was tempered with concern. "I just hope this isn't too much too soon."

"She'll be fine," I said.

"Yeah, but I have a feeling her whole life is about to change."

Scarlett had been in Los Angeles pursuing the acting thing for a while now. She had her ups and downs, starring in a low-budget horror film that never got released. Topless photos from the set were leaked on the Internet. She had dealt with the tabloids, crazy stalkers, and invasive paparazzi—all within the span of the year.

With the release of *Bree*, and her upcoming role in *Ultra Mega 2*, odds were good that Scarlett would become a household name by the end of the summer blockbuster season.

As far as I could tell, she'd been keeping her nose clean and hadn't relapsed. Los Angeles can be a dangerous place for a person with a history of substance abuse. Everything is available and at your fingertips, especially when you're a rising star.

This was a once-in-a-lifetime opportunity. A door that opened quickly and could close at any moment. All it would take was a few missteps. I figured she had enough life experience under her belt to recognize that now. At least, that was my hope.

We left the station and grabbed lunch at *Diver Down*.

Teagan greeted us with a smile as we sat at the bar. "What's shaking?"

"Same ol', same ol'," JD said.

She dug two ice-cold longnecks from the tub and popped the tops with a hiss. She slid them across the counter.

"You read my mind," JD said, reaching for the bottle.

She frowned. "I think it's coming back."

JD lifted a curious brow. "What's coming back? Your *psychic powers?*"

"Don't mock me. I saw on the news you guys found a body in a steel drum. It was a girl, wasn't it?"

"Did they say that on the news?" I asked.

"No, but I had a vision flash in my head. Not a pleasant one, either."

"You wouldn't happen to know who the girl is? That didn't flash into your head, too, did it?"

She frowned at me. "No, it doesn't work like that. And I'd prefer that it didn't work at all."

There always seemed to be dire consequences when Teagan used her supposed psychic abilities.

"Do you guys know what you want for lunch?"

"The question is do you?" JD teased.

"Shut up," she sneered.

"Seafood platter," JD said.

"Crawfish étouffée," I added.

"Coming right up." Teagan punched in the order.

We sipped our beer and shot the breeze. The trailer for the Bree Taylor project played three times on the flatscreen behind the bar during the course of lunch. The studio was doing a big marketing push.

Teagan freaked out when she saw it. "Oh, my God! Is that Scarlett!?"

Jack grinned from ear to ear. "My greatest achievement."

"I'll say. She looks stunning. Are you sure you're related?"

JD frowned at her.

My agent called during the meal. I hadn't talked to him in a while. I figured I'd be hearing from him soon.

I liked Joel. He was one of the good guys in a business that was filled with sharks and vipers. I had become an accidental participant in the business. My chance encounter with Bree turned into a whirlwind of studio meetings and story deals.

"Unless you've been living under a rock, I'm sure you've seen the trailer by now," Joel said.

"I have."

"Fantastic, isn't it?"

"It really is. I'm impressed."

"The studio is being very tight about the project. No pre-screenings. No advanced press screenings."

"What does that mean?"

"It can be good, it can be bad. If the film is a stinker, they certainly don't want the press to get advanced screenings."

I frowned. "You think it's a stinker? The trailer looks great."

"It wouldn't be the first crappy movie with a great trailer," Joel said.

I cringed.

"That said, all of my sources tell me it's fantastic."

"Do you trust your sources?"

"I don't trust anybody. But I've acquired a good nose for bull-shit. So, I'm pretty confident that we've got something that could be an awards contender here. Whether it does well at the box office is another story. Time will tell."

"Fingers crossed," I said.

"The studio's gonna fly you guys out, put you up, all the usual perks. There will be pre-parties and after-parties. You guys will have a blast. David Cameron has finished post-production on Ultra Mega 2. They're dropping the first trailer next week, and the premiere is a month after the Bree Taylor project. You're gonna have a pretty crazy summer. David's gonna take a little time off, then he wants to go full-speed ahead with the television show."

"Sounds good to me."

"I'll touch base soon. Things are about to get exciting," Joel said before ending the call.

We finished eating and headed over to *Mega Music*. The music store contained every instrument and recording gadget known to man. We had the afternoon to kill until band practice, and this was a pretty good way to spend the time. Rows and rows of guitars hung on the walls in all colors: Ferrari Red, Neon Green, Jet Black, and more. There were stacks of amps and cabinets. Drums and cymbals. A recording section was home to high-end microphones, keyboards, and speakers.

"This is great," JD said, "but I don't need to spend anymore money here."

"Don't worry. I'm the one spending money today."

7

I made a beeline for the bass guitars. After all the drama we'd been through recently with Crash breaking his wrist and needing to find a temporary replacement, I figured it was a good idea to pick up a cheap bass guitar and start practicing—just in case we ever got into a bind again. Plus, I had to admit, the one time that I *did* jam with the band, it was fun.

I had done some research online, and I knew what I wanted. I grabbed a cheap Squire Mini Precision Bass from the rack, found an amp, and plugged in.

The bass was finished in gloss black and had a maple fretboard. The mini bass was smaller than a regular P-Bass, and that was fine by me. I just needed something to noodle around on in my stateroom. I figured with a little practice, I'd be able to hold down a groove. And for a couple hundred bucks, I couldn't go wrong.

I plucked the strings and started playing a *Wild Fury* song that Crash had taught me.

JD chuckled. "I see where this is going."

"We need backup systems in place," I said.

We always planned for contingencies on the battlefield but had been woefully underprepared when it came to the band. We were all flying by the seat of our pants. As manager, I decided it was probably a good idea to start making plans for every possible scenario. If it *can* go wrong, it probably *will* at some point.

I fumbled through the song, and JD sang along. It put a smile on both of our faces.

I liked the guitar. It felt good in my hands. I gave it a look over for blemishes or other defects that might give me a little negotiating room on the price. There were fingerprints all over it. It had been pawed on by more teenage boys than the prom queen.

I unplugged it, grabbed the small practice amp, and carted them both up to the counter.

The pasty-faced salesclerk with hair that fell into his eyes tried to upsell me on a hard case. But since the bass came with a nice soft case, I declined the offer. This wasn't a collector's instrument. I didn't care if it got beat up. Besides, dings and scratches would give it more character. People pay good money for *relic'd* guitars. Kind of like buying jeans with holes in them—you pay more for the holes.

The amp was small enough to fit in the front trunk of the Porsche, and I slid the guitar into the backseat. We cruised to the warehouse district and pulled into the parking lot of the practice studio.

The rumble of a band playing inside filtered into the parking area.

We hopped out of the car, and I grabbed the bass guitar. JD clicked the alarm, and the lights flashed.

I left the practice amp in the trunk. Nobody knew it was in there, and I didn't think much of leaving it. I slung the soft case over my shoulder and headed toward the main entrance.

The usual band of miscreants hung outside, smoking cigarettes and wasting time. There were plenty of pasty faces, dyed jet black hair, eyeliner, and studded bracelets. Somehow, despite living in the sunshine capital of the world, these kids managed to see less daylight than your average vampire.

"Yo, what's up, Thrash," one of them said, lifting his hand to high-five.

Thrash was JD's stage name.

JD smacked his palm, returning the gesture. "Rock 'n' roll!"

"Alright, alright!"

We pushed inside the warehouse and ambled down the dim hallway. As usual, the lingering smell of illicit herbal substances filled the air.

The band was tuning up as we pushed into the practice space. Styxx was behind his candy-apple red drum set, adjusting the toms. Dizzy was on guitar, his fingers racing up and down the fretboard. Faye thumped out a groove on her bass. The sultry little vixen had one more show with the band. Crash would be getting his cast off any day now. We'd cut it off once before when we got in a bind, but he'd been warned not to remove the second one prematurely.

I glanced around and noticed that he was conspicuously absent. There were two groupies on the couch.

"Where's Crash?" I asked.

Dizzy shrugged.

My eyes flicked to Styxx, and he repeated the gesture. "I don't know. Why don't you ask Faye?"

There was more than a hint of disdain in his voice.

"Don't look at me," Faye replied. "I'm not his keeper."

Despite the rules JD had put down, the two had a little something going on. JD didn't have any room to talk, having broken the rules himself.

Crash was head over heels.

And what guy in Crash's position wouldn't be?

I got the impression that Faye didn't respond to Crash with quite the same enthusiasm.

Faye was an alluring little platinum blonde with a short pixie cut and pigtails. She wore a tight tank top cut up to accentuate her assets, and her short miniskirt sparked naughty desires. She wore tall Dr. Martens and was an alternative rock princess. She was quite captivating in a dangerous, life on the edge, rock 'n' roll kind of way.

I pulled my phone from my pocket and called Crash's cell number. After a few rings, it went to voicemail. "Hey, where are you? We're about to start practice. Call me back."

Despite having the cast on his arm for the last six weeks, Crash never missed practice. He was always there, cheering on the band—even when he had to sit on the sidelines for their biggest show.

Wild Fury was his life.

My suspicious eyes turned to Faye. "Is there something you're not telling me?"

"Like what?" she asked innocently.

"Is there some specific reason that Crash would be avoiding practice and my phone calls?"

She looked at her fretboard and continued to noodle, shifting uncomfortably. "I don't know what you want me to say, man. I don't know where he is."

"When was the last time you talked to him?"

She shrugged. "A couple days ago."

"I thought you two were close."

"Excuse me, what business is it of yours?" she snapped.

"I get concerned when a member of the band doesn't show up," I said.

"Look, did we come here to jam or not?"

"Let's do it," JD said.

"We worked up a new groove," Dizzy said. "Styxx has got lyrics ready to go and everything. Let's try it out."

Styxx handed JD a crumpled piece of paper with lyrics scribbled all over it. JD studied the incomprehensible mess and somehow made sense of it.

I wondered how Crash would feel about the guys writing a song without him.

Styxx clicked off the beat, and Faye and Dizzy thundered in, laying down a heavy groove. JD bobbed his head, listening to the music, getting a feel for it. They played the verse and the chorus, and when they circled back around to the verse again, JD belted out the lyrics in a high-pitched howl.

I grinned.

It had potential from the first bar—these guys had something special, there was no doubt about it. They ran through the song a couple times, working out the bugs. JD played with the phrasing here and there. By the fourth or fifth time, it sounded polished.

Curious onlookers filtered into the room, looking for a free show. The band ran through their setlist and wrapped up 45 minutes later.

By the time it was over, the place was packed. The band was lauded with raucous applause and cheers. There was that vibe in the air, and everyone around knew they were witnessing something special—on the ground floor as *Wild Fury* built a name for themselves. As the opening act for Chloe-C in New York, they had cemented their reputation on a national stage as a hard-hitting party rock band that could put on a hell of a live show.

I just hoped things weren't about to implode.

8

B and practice was never just *practice*. There was always an after-party. As usual, we ended up at *Tide Pool* with JD buying the drinks. Harper, at the outdoor bar, kept the drinks flowing, and JD handed them out. He raised his glass to toast, "Good times and good friends!"

We all clinked glasses and sipped our beverages.

I tried calling Crash again, but it went to voicemail. I checked my phone for missed calls or texts, but he hadn't replied.

I pulled Faye aside. "Do I need to be concerned about him?"

She shrugged.

"Look, I know it's none of my business, but it's sort of my business. What's going on with you two?"

She stared me down for a moment, took a deep breath, then let out a long exhale. "Okay, look... I like Crash. I really do. But he's trying to move this thing along way too fast. I mean, he professed his love for me the other day. How am I supposed to respond to that?"

"Crash is a good guy."

"I know he is." She frowned. "I feel terrible. I'm just not ready for a relationship yet. It's too much for me to think about at the moment. I want to play my bass, have fun, and I don't want to answer to anybody. I don't want to become somebody's possession. I don't want to have to pick up the phone when I don't want to pick up the phone."

"I get it. You're young. This is the time of your life."

"It is. I told him I wasn't ready for a committed relationship, and that wasn't what he wanted to hear. We haven't spoken since. I think he's probably pretty hurt and pissed off." She frowned again. "You met my last boyfriend. Complete jerk. Controlling, manipulative, cheater. I'm just not in a position where I can get vulnerable again."

"Don't project your last boyfriend onto Crash. He's not *that* guy."

"I know. I know."

"I get it. If you don't get close, you don't get hurt."

She nodded.

"But don't let a good thing pass you by because you're scared."

Her face twisted as she thought about it. "I know. You're right. But I just can't fall in love on someone else's timeline. I really like Crash. Like, a lot. But I can't say that I'm in love with him right now. That's not to say that I might not be in the future. But I just want to take things one day at a time and see how it goes. I mean, I'm not that girl that you give me one good orgasm and I'm head over heels. Doesn't work like that for me."

I chuckled. "As long as you guys are straight up with each other. That's all you can do. Just don't play games. Don't lead him on. Don't break his heart."

"I already broke his heart." Her face crinkled with disappointment. She was silent for a long moment. "You really care about these guys, don't you?"

"Yeah, I do. This little band of misfits is like a second family to me. And JD is like a brother."

Faye smiled, "They're lucky to have you looking out for them."

She lifted her glass, and we toasted.

"One more show," she said.

"One more show."

We sipped our whiskey.

"You're gonna be so glad when I'm gone, aren't you?" she muttered.

"I'm eternally thankful for what you've done for the band, and I'm in awe of your talent."

"A diplomatic answer."

I smiled. "I'm looking forward to things getting back to normal."

She laughed. "Normal? Is there such a thing, really?"

I chuckled. "No. You're probably right."

"You give good advice," JD said, having caught the tail end of it. "Maybe you should listen to yourself?"

I rolled my eyes.

My phone buzzed my pocket. I snatched the device and looked at the screen. It had to be bad news. I answered the call, and the sheriff grumbled through gritted teeth. His voice was tight, almost on the verge of breaking up. "I need you and JD to get over to the corner of Sunbeam and Pearl ASAP! Officer down."

My stomach twisted with dread, and I grimaced. I didn't even want to ask who.

"Chuck Atwood's been shot."

"We're on it. What condition is he in?"

9

The area swarmed with patrol units and first responders. Red and blue lights flickered. Just about every deputy in the department was on the scene. Sunbeam Street had two lanes each way, divided by a median. Homes on either side were set off from the street with a brick wall and lots of foliage. I hoped that someone had seen or heard something.

JD parked the Porsche at the curb. We hopped out and weaved through the sea of first responders.

Chuck's body lay on the asphalt near his patrol car, both riddled with bullets. Crimson soaked his polyester uniform.

He wasn't breathing anymore.

EMTs and paramedics had attempted to revive him, but Chuck was long gone by the time they arrived.

Bullet holes dotted the door and quarter panel of his patrol cruiser.

Neighbors gawked at the gruesome scene.

Deputies canvassed the area for witnesses.

The sheriff's face was red and his jaw tight. His eyes were misty, so mad he didn't know whether to scream or cry.

"What do we know?" I asked.

"Routine traffic stop. He called in the plates on a red Honda that is registered to Justin Kessler. 22 years old. I've got a BOLO out on the suspect now. Erickson and Faulkner are waiting at the kid's apartment for him to turn up." Daniels shook his head. "Chuck pulled the kid over for a busted tail light. 30 years on the job and a busted tail light gets you killed."

He hung his head and sighed.

"Any witnesses?"

The sheriff shook his head. "Not so far. Couple of the neighbors said they heard multiple gunshots, then tires squeal."

The forensics guys were examining the roadway, looking for tire tracks. Cameras flashed as they photographed the area.

"When did this happen?" I asked.

"He called in the stop about 45 minutes ago," Daniels said.

"What do we know about the driver of the vehicle, Justin Kessler?"

"No criminal history. Graduated Coconut Key High School. Took some classes at the community college."

A news van arrived on the scene, the station logo emblazoned on the side. Paris Delaney and crew hopped out and hustled toward us. The camera lens soaked up the scene.

"Have you talked to Ellie yet?" I asked the sheriff.

"No. That's an *in-person* conversation." He frowned. "I want you two to find out who did this and bring them to justice. I don't care how you have to do it."

I gave him a grim nod.

My eyes flicked to Paris Delaney. For once, I was glad to see her.

I left the sheriff and marched toward the beautiful blonde. She saw me coming and nudged the cameraman. The lens swung in my direction.

"Deputy Wild, what can you tell us?"

"This evening, about 10:15 PM, a Coconut County deputy was shot and killed during a routine traffic stop on Sunbeam near Pearl. If anyone has information about the crime, please contact the Coconut County Sheriff's Department immediately. Thank you."

I turned around and left the news crew.

"Deputy Wild, has the name of the officer been released?"

I ignored her and rejoined JD and Sheriff Daniels. We watched as Chuck was put into a body bag and loaded into the medical examiner's van.

"I guess I better break the bad news to Ellie," Daniels said.

A call from the dispatch unit crackled over his walkie-talkie. He pushed the talk button. "This is Daniels. Go ahead."

"A patrol unit just picked up Justin Kessler. He was with a passenger. Both are being transported to the station."

"I'm on my way."

We left the scene and hustled back to JD's Porsche. We sped to the station.

After Justin was processed and printed, he was put into an interrogation room. There were plenty of deputies that wanted 5 minutes alone with the kid. Cop killers didn't get treated too kindly around here. The kid was lucky he didn't have an *accident* on the way to the station.

JD and I pushed into the interrogation room. Justin didn't strike me as a cop killer. There was nothing in his record to indicate violence. But people do strange things when they're hopped up on illicit substances.

Justin had blond hair trimmed short on the sides and long on top. The sun had bleached the tips. His face was somewhere in-between round and narrow, and his sad brown eyes drooped in the corners. He still had some teen acne, and his hairline was rapidly receding, despite his young age. His eyes were red and glassy, clearly stoned.

"Want to tell me what happened?"

"I don't know what happened," Justin said. "All of a sudden, there were flashing lights in my rearview mirror. These two deputies pulled me over, hassled us. Now I'm here, talking to you."

I asked, "No. What happened before the deputies arrested you?"

He was silent for a long moment.

"You know, when the first officer pulled you over," I said in a condescending tone. "Deputy Chuck Atwood. The guy that's dead."

Justin's eyes rounded. "He's dead?"

"That's what happens when you fill somebody full of bullets."

"I didn't do that. I swear!"

"So, I'm going to ask you again. What happened?"

He exhaled. "The first cop pulled me over for a busted tail light. He gave me a warning and let me go. As he was heading back to the patrol car, these guys pulled up and shot him."

"Who?"

"I don't know who."

"Tell me about them."

"Two guys. They wore ski masks. They drove by and blasted your friend with a submachine gun. It was crazy."

"What were they driving?"

"A silver car."

"Two-door, or four-door?"

Justin shrugged. "I don't know. I think it was a four-door."

"And you just took off?"

"Yeah. I was scared shitless. I didn't know if those guys were gonna come back or what. I got the hell out of there."

"You can't just leave the scene of a crime like that."

"I was scared those guys were gonna kill me too."

"And you didn't bother to report the incident?"

He exhaled and slumped. "Man, I didn't want anything to do with that. I mean, what if those guys come after me?"

I frowned and exchanged a glance with JD.

"When you were arrested, Deputies Erickson and Faulkner found a bag of weed and paraphernalia in your car. Your blood alcohol level was 1.2, well beyond the legal limit. You mean to tell me that Deputy Atwood was just going to let you go with a warning?"

"Yeah. I swear!"

I didn't buy it for a second. "What else can you tell me about the shooters?"

Justin shrugged. "I don't know. It all happened so fast."

"You get a license plate?"

"No. I was too freaked out."

"Who's the girl in the car with you?"

"Kennedy?"

"Yeah. She your girlfriend?"

His face tightened, and he clammed up. "She's just a friend."

"She's 17."

"So?"

"You're 22. You're an adult. She's not."

"Aw, come on, dude. She's close enough."

"Close enough doesn't count."

"I didn't touch her. I swear. We're just friends."

Another line that I didn't believe. "Right. *Friends*. As it stands, you're looking at possession of a controlled substance, DUI, which is compounded by the fact you had a minor in the car."

"She's 17!" he protested. "Have you seen her? She doesn't look 17." His eyes flicked between the two of us, looking for sympathy. "I'm not going to jail, am I?"

"That's what happens when you break the law," I said in monotone.

"But I'm a prosecution witness. I can testify against the shooters if you catch them."

"That's something you can work out with the DA."

He frowned. "Does that mean I gotta spend the night in jail?"

"You'll stay in jail until somebody bails you out. You'll get arraigned in the morning."

"What does that mean?"

"You'll go before the judge. If you can think of anything else about the shooters, let us know. If you help us, it might help your case."

I pushed away from the table and stepped to the door.

Justin hung his head and sighed.

A guard buzzed us out, and we stepped into the hallway.

Daniels joined us a moment later, having watched the interrogation from the observation room. "I'll put a BOLO out on the silver sedan. Talk to the girl and see if her story matches."

"Will do," I said.

We walked down the hall and pushed into interrogation room #2.

Kennedy fidgeted nervously. She was a pretty girl. Shoulder-length dark hair, heavy eye shadow, piercing blue eyes, and a black choker around her neck. She definitely had the angsty teen thing going on. Hanging out with a loser like Justin probably had the desired effect of pissing off her parents.

"I'm not in any kind of trouble, am I?" she asked innocently. "I mean, you're not gonna tell my parents, are you?"

"That depends," I said.

"On what?"

"How cooperative you are."

She looked at me and swallowed hard.

"Is Justin your boyfriend?"

She shrugged tentatively. "I mean, we hang out."

"He takes you out and gets you high?"

She shook her head. "I don't smoke."

Judging by the condition of her eyes, I would say she was lying. "I thought you were gonna cooperate."

"I'm not going to admit to doing something illegal. Do I look stupid?"

"Well, your choice of friends leaves a little to be desired."

She scowled at me.

"Are you engaged in a sexual relationship with Justin?"

"No. Perv!"

I rolled my eyes. Probably another lie. "You're a pretty girl. You can do better than Justin."

She didn't disagree.

"Tell me about the traffic stop," I said.

She pretty much told me the same story. Two guys in a silver sedan, wearing ski masks with a submachine gun.

"I told him we need to report it," she said, "but Justin didn't want to say anything. He was afraid we'd get in trouble. And it appears that we are."

"Did you get a look at the license plate?"

She shook her head. "It was kind of surreal. I heard the gunshots, and it took me a second to process what was happening. I looked through the back window and saw them gun the cop down. I was stunned. I just watched them pass by. The two killers glared at us, and I ducked in my seat. I really thought they were going to shoot us for a second. Then they took off. Justin started the car, and we got the hell out of there." She paused. "I'm really sorry about your friend."

Kennedy was a sharp kid. I couldn't tell if she was saying that just to get on our good side or if it was sincere. Maybe a little of both.

"Do your parents know where you are?" I asked.

"My parents don't care where I am." She paused. "What's gonna happen to Justin?"

"He's going to get charged with several misdemeanors."

"Will he do jail time?"

I shrugged.

"What about me?"

"Have you been drinking?"

She shook her head.

I lifted my brow.

"A couple of beers," she admitted.

"You're too young to drink beer."

"Like you guys never did the same thing."

JD and I exchanged a glance.

"I'm gonna call your parents to come pick you up."

She frowned. "Do you have to? Can't you just give me a ride home and drop me off, and we'll call it even? It's just gonna start a lot of unnecessary drama."

She looked at me with sad, pouty eyes, pleading for a break.

11

I had Mendoza run the girl home. I strongly urged her to reconsider her life choices. She was about to turn 18 in two weeks, and any trouble she got into would stick with her. It was pretty clear she wasn't going to rat out Justin at this point.

Every patrol unit on the island was looking for the silver sedan. We cruised around for an hour with our eyes peeled. With no luck, we eventually left it to the patrol units and headed back to *Diver Down*.

"I heard about the shooting on the news," Teagan said. "You guys have any leads?"

I frowned and shook my head.

"I'm really sorry."

"Thanks."

We ordered a drink, and JD lifted his glass. "To Chuck."

We clinked glasses and sipped the whiskey. It was hard to believe Chuck was gone. The gravity of it hadn't fully sunk in yet. JD and I were in a somber mood as we nursed our drinks.

We called it an early night. JD headed home, and I ambled down the dock. I crossed the passerelle to the aft deck and slid open the door to the salon. Buddy greeted me with excitement. He was a bright spot in an otherwise dreary evening.

I grabbed his leash and took him out for a quick walk before bed. I tossed and turned all night, thinking about Chuck, dreaming about the incident, helpless to stop it.

Chuck was one of those guys you couldn't help but like. Anytime someone in the department went down, we all felt it. It could happen to any of us at anytime.

I pulled myself out of bed in the morning as the sun blasted through the windows. That uneasy feeling from the night before still lingered. Something was wrong with the world, and there was no way to make it right.

I took Buddy out for a run. Despite having a sleepless night, I had restless energy to burn off. I came back to the boat, fixed breakfast, and tried to shake off the gloomy feeling.

Daniels called. "We got a report this morning of a stolen car. Silver four-door sedan. Belongs to a woman named Norah Griffith. Says she stepped out of her house for work this morning and the car wasn't where she'd left it. I'll let you know if and when it turns up, but I'm guessing that's the vehicle the shooters used."

"Keep me posted. Have you talked to Ellie?"

"I paid her a visit and broke the news to her last night. All things considered, she took it pretty well, or at least, she put on a good front. I tell you, if I never have to do that again, that'd be just fine with me."

"I understand."

"I told her you boys would be over sometime today. Talk to her. See if you can piece this thing together. I'm of the mind that this wasn't a random shooting. Start poking around. Find out who wanted Chuck dead."

"I'm on it."

I took a shower, got dressed, and grabbed my weapon from the nightstand drawer. I press checked it and holstered it in my waistband for an appendix carry.

I called JD, and he swung by the marina 15 minutes later to pick me up. I jogged down the dock and hopped into the passenger seat of the Miami Blue Porsche. We drove across the island, the morning sun beaming down.

Chuck and Ellie had a nice one-story home on Bloom Street. It was surrounded by a white picket fence and two large fan palm trees that shrouded the house. It was painted in mint green.

We parked at the curb, pushed through the gate, and climbed the steps to the front porch. I shared a glance with JD and took a deep breath before knocking on the door.

Ellie pulled it open a few moments later.

"I'm so sorry for your loss," I said.

She forced a grim smile and nodded. "Thank you. Come on in." She held the door and motioned for us to enter. We stepped into the foyer, and she closed the door behind us.

Ellie was normally a bubbly and vivacious blonde, but now she was a red-nosed, puffy-eyed mess. She looked like she hadn't slept, and she had a tissue in her hand in case an emergency rush of tears flooded from her eyes.

Ellie was 43—quite a bit younger than Chuck. But their age difference didn't seem to matter.

She escorted us into the living room and offered us a seat on the couch.

Her wavy hair hung at shoulder length. She had a slender face, brown eyes, and pouty lips. She was girl-next-door pretty. Wholesome. The kind of woman you built a life with.

"Please tell me you know who did this," she said.

"We're doing everything we can," I assured. "Is there anyone you can think of that we should be looking at?"

She shook her head. "You know Chuck. He got along with everybody."

"Did he express any concern about his open cases?"

"He didn't really bring home his work. He felt it was better to leave the job at the office. He didn't talk about it, and I didn't ask. Every now and then he might say something, but he really didn't want to blend the two worlds."

"How were things between you two?"

"They were great. I mean, we were about to enter the biggest transitional phase of our lives."

"He mentioned wanting to move to Montana," I said

She rolled her eyes. "I don't know what he was thinking. I mean, if that's what he really wanted to do, I would have done it. But I don't think that's what he really wanted. It's one of those things that sounds good when you talk about it. I think he liked the idea of becoming a rancher and living out some type of western fantasy. But I think he would have changed his mind at the first hard freeze."

"I hate to ask, but I gotta do my due diligence."

Ellie nodded.

"Did he owe anybody money? Gambling debts? Anything like that?"

"Not that I know of."

"Was he having any type of affair?"

She chortled. "No. I was enough for Chuck. I don't think he had the time or the energy."

"What about you?"

She sighed. "I know this is standard stuff, and you've got to ask, but no."

The room was silent for a moment.

"Is there anything you need? Anything we can do?"

"Besides get the bastards who did this? No. I'm coasting along on autopilot." She sighed again. "It hasn't really sunk in yet. I'm not allowing myself to go there. If I let it consume me, I may never get up again. I gotta get through the next couple weeks, get everything taken care of, then I can mourn."

She blotted her eyes as they misted.

"You never think you're gonna be the one," she said as she started to break down. "I know this is gonna sound terrible, but I can't tell you the number of times the department lost a deputy, and my first thought was *thank God that wasn't Chuck*. Now I'm the grieving widow."

She was silent for a moment. Then the waterworks started.

"One day," she sobbed. "He just had to make it one more day. I was so nervous for the last two weeks. I just had this terrible feeling, but I bit my tongue and told myself I was just being paranoid."

"There's nothing you could have done to change this," I said.

"I could have stopped him from going to work." Her head fell into her hands, and she sobbed, her chest jerking.

It's terrible to watch someone in pain, knowing there's nothing you can do for them.

She cried it out for a moment, blew her nose, wiped her eyes with a fresh tissue, and took a deep breath. "Look at me, I'm falling apart. And I promised myself I'd keep it together."

"You gotta let it out when it needs to come out," I said. "Holding it back is the worst thing you can do."

"I know," she sniffled. "I can hear Chuck now, telling me to stop, saying that crying ain't gonna bring him back."

"Again, my deepest condolences," I said. "If there is anything you need, don't hesitate to call. Anytime. Day or night. We're gonna do everything we can to find out who did this. If you can think of anything..."

"I'll let you know." She forced a grim smile. "Thank you for stopping by. Chuck was really fond of you both."

We said our goodbyes and showed ourselves out. We ambled down the walkway and pushed through the gate.

"That's just gut-wrenching," JD said as he slipped behind the wheel.

He cranked up the engine, and Brenda called as we pulled away from the curb.

"Tell me you've got something," I said.

"I do."

12

"This is pretty messed up," Brenda said. Messed up was par for the course in Coconut Key. "The girl in the barrel was approximately 16 to 17 years old."

I winced.

"That's not all. She wasn't alone."

There certainly weren't two adults in that barrel. "She was pregnant?"

"Bingo."

I cringed again.

"From what I can tell, this type of barrel was manufactured during the '70s and '80s. That specific barrel isn't manufactured anymore."

"So this is a cold case?"

"Looks that way. From what I can tell, there are no recent missing persons that match this victim in this area. Doesn't mean she wasn't killed somewhere else and transported down here. Who knows where she came from. I talked to the chemical company listed on the barrel, and they are looking through their database. Since the barrel is so old, those records are not on their computer, so someone is flipping through a file cabinet as we speak. Hopefully, those records haven't been tossed out."

"What about the identity of the girl?"

"I'm working on that, but I need somewhere to start first. The bad news is that the sodium hydroxide dissolved all the flesh and fibrous materials. Good news is that some of the acrylic fibers and thermoplastics remained intact."

"So, there were other items in the barrel with her?"

"Yes. She had a bookbag with her. Most of the bag and its contents were destroyed. But one of the textbooks had a cover that was coated with a thermoplastic resin. It's pretty faded and damaged, but with a spectroscope, I might be able to pick out some details of the cover, hopefully the title and edition number. I might be able to track down when and where that book was used."

"Fingers crossed."

"Also, I didn't find any evidence of a cell phone. At least some of the components would have survived the sodium hydroxide. That tells me we could be dealing with a very old case. How many teenagers do you know that are separated from their phone? Again, nothing conclusive. The girl's killer could have disposed of that somewhere else."

"Keep me posted."

"Will do," she said before ending the call.

JD drove to the station, and we hopped out and pushed inside. The office bustled with activity. JD and I poured ourselves a cup of coffee, then found Denise at her desk.

"Do me a favor, would you?" I asked.

"Depends on the favor," she sassed.

"Start sifting through all of Chuck's recent arrests. Let's start putting together a list of potential suspects who may have had a vendetta."

"I'm already on it," she said with a smile.

I grinned.

Daniels stepped out of his office and marched toward us. "Mendoza just pulled over a silver sedan with plates that match the stolen vehicle. He's at the 400 block of Pompano Drive. Get over there and see what you can find out. I'm sending a forensics team to go over the vehicle with a fine-toothed comb."

We hustled out of the station and ran across the parking lot to the Porsche. We hopped in the car and sped over to the scene.

The lights on Mendoza's patrol car flickered behind the silver sedan that was pulled to the shoulder near a self-storage unit. A brunette woman in her late 20s stood by the trunk of the vehicle with Mendoza. We parked behind the patrol car and hopped out.

Mendoza shook his head as we approached. "No dice. This isn't the car. Somebody swapped the plates. The VIN doesn't match."

"I didn't even notice," the woman said. "I swear, I didn't shoot a cop. I don't even own a gun."

Her name was April McGee. She said she worked at a daycare for special needs children. She didn't quite fit the profile of a cop killer. She had shoulder-length brown hair, a pretty face, and wore a plain sundress. Mendoza had run a background check on her, and she had no criminal history. No outstanding warrants. Not so much as a speeding ticket.

"Where were you last night around 10 PM?" I asked.

"I was at home," April said. "I go to sleep pretty early. I'm usually out by 10 or 10:30 PM."

"What about your car?"

"It was parked on the street last night."

"You didn't happen to see anyone switch the plates, did you?"

She shook her head, then thought for a moment. "But I do have a video doorbell. It goes off every time somebody on the street passes by. I've been meaning to turn the sensitivity down."

I exchanged an optimistic glance with JD.

April pulled her phone from her purse and launched the monitoring app. She scrolled through the history and scanned several clips. Most of them were cars passing by, people walking on the streets, kids riding bicycles. Around dusk, there was a clip of a kid who rode his bike up to the car with a license plate in his hand. He unscrewed the plate from April's car and swapped it out, then rode away.

"Can you export that clip and send it to me?" I asked.

She nodded and did so.

The video file buzzed my phone a moment later. I replayed it again and zoomed in, but it became pixelated with magnification.

"Do you recognize this kid?"

She nodded. "I don't know his name, but I see him playing with the kid down the street, Ben." Her face crinkled. "Why would he swap plates?"

13

"Swapping plates with your car makes it less likely that the perps get pulled over since the cars look the same and your car hasn't been reported stolen," I said.

"Makes sense," she replied.

"Can you tell me where Ben lives?"

"Sure thing. He's just down the street from me." She gave me the address. "What do I do about the license plates?"

"You need to get new plates," Mendoza said. "You can't drive the car without them."

The forensics team arrived, removed the stolen plates from the vehicle, and dusted them for fingerprints.

We left the scene and headed to Ben's house. He lived a few blocks away on Parnell Street in a teal, two-story house. There was a low concrete wall around the front yard with a wrought-iron gate. There were various types of palm trees in the yard.

We parked at the curb, hopped out, and pushed through the gate. We banged on the white double doors.

"Who is it?" a female voice asked through the door.

"Coconut County, ma'am." I held up my badge as she peered through a side window.

She pulled open the door with a curious look on her face. She was in her late 30s and had wavy brown hair that hung to her shoulders.

"We're looking for a boy that lives in the neighborhood. He's friends with your son, Ben." I showed her a screengrab of the suspect's image. "You recognize this kid?"

"I can't be totally sure, but that looks like Jared. What's he done?"

I filled her in on the situation.

She looked mortified. "You don't think Ben had anything to do with this, do you?"

"Hard to say, ma'am. My guess is that someone got the kid to swap out the plates. How old is your son?"

"Ben is 12, and I think Jared is either 12 or 13."

"Do you know where Jared lives?"

"He lives in a duplex around the corner, but I'm not sure of the exact address. I can give you his mother's phone number if you need it."

"That would be helpful."

She texted it to me after I gave her my number.

"What's Jared's last name?"

"Landis."

"Thank you. Do me a favor and keep this between us until we have a chance to talk to Jared. Please don't contact his mother."

She nodded.

I thanked her for the information and headed back down the walkway. We pushed through the gate and stepped onto the sidewalk. I called Denise at the station and asked her to pull up background information on Jared Landis. The kid was a student at the middle school. He didn't have a juvenile record, but his brother did.

Trevor was 17 and had quite an impressive start. He was about to turn 18 in a few days. His budding career included burglary, assault, and possession. Two of his recent arrests were made by Deputy Chuck Atwood.

The dots were starting to connect.

We hopped into the car and zipped around the corner to the duplex.

"Coconut County," I shouted when I banged on the door.

According to the records, Jared and his brother lived with their mother, Janice. The duplex was a small white house with two red doors and red shutters. A white picket fence surrounded the lawn, but oddly there were no trees. It looked barren compared to the surrounding lawns.

Janice pulled open the door with a tight face and annoyed eyes. "Which one are you here for?"

"Both," I said.

She stifled a groan.

Janice had short dark hair, brown eyes, and a narrow face. She was mid to late 30s and had a petite figure.

"What did they do now?"

I showed her the video footage.

She cringed.

"Is that your son?"

I could see the torment in her eyes. "That image is really grainy. It's difficult to say."

I gave her a flat stare. "Come on, Mrs. Landis. It's Jared."

"What's this about?"

"One of our deputies was shot and killed. The suspects were driving a stolen car. We believe the plates of the stolen car were swapped with a vehicle owned by April McGee. We don't think Jared was involved in the shooting. But we want to know why he swapped the plates and who else was involved."

Concern bathed her eyes.

A yellow school bus squealed to a stop nearby. The brakes hissed, and the flashing red lights flickered. School kids flooded off the bus, wearing backpacks and carrying books, eager to indulge in an afternoon of play.

It was a bunch of middle school kids, and it didn't take long for Jared to emerge from the crowd. He marched toward the duplex and hesitated when he caught sight of us at the front door. We all stared in his direction.

He contemplated taking off and running. He knew he was in some kind of trouble. After a moment's pause, he kept marching forward. Jared stepped onto the porch and gave us a curious look. "Who are you?"

"These two deputies would like to talk to you," Janice said in a stern tone.

Jared's suspicious eyes flicked to us. "You don't look like cops."

I flashed my badge.

"Am I supposed to be scared?"

"You got something to be scared about?"

"Nope."

"Is this you?" I said, showing him the image on my phone.

He studied it briefly. "Nope."

I lifted an incredulous brow. "Really?"

"Nope."

I played the full video for him. "That's not you exchanging the plates on the car."

He shook his head. "Nope. That ain't me. Doesn't even look like me."

"It looks an awful lot like you."

"I don't know what to tell you."

"You could tell me who asked you to swap the plates."

"I told you. That ain't me."

"Did your brother ask you to do it?"

Jared shook his head.

"Where is Trevor?" I asked Janice.

She looked at her watch. "He should be getting home from school any minute now. If he bothered to go."

"Jared, you're not gonna get in any trouble if you cooperate with us," I said. "We just need to know who asked you to swap the plates."

Maybe I was being naïve, but I didn't figure a 12-year-old kid would gun down a deputy sheriff. Then again, we were living in strange times.

"I want to talk to my attorney," Jared said.

"You're not under arrest," I said.

A car full of kids pulled to the curb in front of the duplex. I recognized Trevor from his mug shot as he hopped out of the backseat. The car drove away, and he walked to the door with caution.

"Don't say anything, Trevor," Jared shouted. "They're cops."

His eyes rounded, and his face tensed. He froze in his tracks.

"We just need to have a few words with you," I said.

14

"You better not have done anything!" Janice snapped. "I'm still trying to pay off the last trouble you got into."

"I didn't do nothing," Trevor said.

"Did you have your little brother swap license plates on April McGee's car?" I asked.

His face crinkled. "No. I don't know what you're talking about."

"Where were you last night around 10 PM?" I asked.

"He was here with me," Janice said. "It was a school night. I don't let the boys out on a school night."

I knew she didn't want to see her kids get in trouble. I wasn't sure if she was just covering for them or if they really were at home like she said.

"I think we've said all we're going to say," Janice said. "You need anything else, come back with a warrant." Her stern gaze snapped to her kids. "Get inside now! Both of you."

They slumped and shuffled into the duplex.

Janice frowned at us and slammed the door. She yelled at both of them once they were inside. "What the hell did you get into this time?"

We stood on the porch and eavesdropped as she berated them.

"I didn't do nothing," Trevor protested.

"You're both grounded."

The kids groaned.

"What for?" Trevor moaned.

"I don't know. But I'm sure you did something to deserve it. Both of you get to your rooms and do your homework.

"I don't have any homework," Jared said.

"Neither do I," Trevor replied.

"I know you're lying now."

We left the porch and walked back to the Porsche.

"Think Trevor is our shooter?" JD asked.

"At this point, I'm not ruling anyone out."

JD frowned and shook his head in disgust. He cranked up the engine and pulled away from the curb. We headed back to the station, filled out paperwork, then talked to Denise.

"I found some interesting leads," she said. Her fingers danced across the keyboard, and a mugshot appeared on the display. "A pimp named Angel Moreno. Chuck arrested him. He's out on bail. Looks like there's some plea deal in the works. He's got a few assaults under his belt. Pimping, pandering. A possession charge."

"Possible." I wasn't sold on the suspect.

"There's another guy Chuck arrested. Isaac Norwood. " Her fingers danced again. "Routine traffic stop. Chuck found 2 kilos of cocaine in the trunk. He was with a guy named Kashton Epps. Looks like they both got off with a non-prosecution agreement and a fine payable to the Coconut Forward Fund."

"Arrested with 2 kilos and they get off with a fine?" I asked in disbelief.

Denise shrugged.

"If they're getting off that light, not much incentive for revenge. What else have you got?"

Her fingers raced across the keyboard again. A mugshot and background information appeared on the screen. "This guy just got out of prison last week. He took an Alford plea. Did 15 years for the rape and murder of Darcy Klien. The guy's name is Felix Yates. Defense claimed the arresting officer planted evidence. Prosecutors got worried he might win the appeal and gave him a deal for time served. He took it."

I exchanged a glance with JD.

"No way Chuck would fabricate evidence," I said, mostly certain of the statement.

Denise shrugged. "The guy had been positively ID'd by two other women that alleged he attacked and assaulted them in the months prior, but prosecutors couldn't make the cases stick, and he walked. Maybe Chuck didn't want to see this guy get off a third time?"

I grimaced. I didn't want to believe Chuck would do something like that.

"I don't know about you," JD said, "but if I got locked up for 15 years for something I didn't do, I'd be pretty pissed off."

"If this is true, Felix Yates had a motive for revenge," I said.

"Yeah, but after 15 years in the can, I wouldn't want to risk going back," Denise said.

"Some people don't think too clearly in the heat of the moment," I said. "Where do we find Felix?"

"He's living at Phoenix House. It's run by a non-profit that assists former inmates with re-integration. According to the records, he's a sacker at the Oceanside Grocery."

"I say we go talk to Felix," JD said.

W e swung by Phoenix House. Felix wasn't there. We finally caught up with him at the Oceanside Grocery, and he wasn't too thrilled to see us. As soon as we flashed our badges, his eyes filled with scorn.

Felix had a permanent scowl etched on his face. He was 63 years old, had a long gray bushy beard, and long gray hair on the sides. The top of his head was cue ball slick. He had ice-blue eyes that, at one point in his life, had been vibrant. Now they were dull and angry. He stuffed groceries into a bag as we talked to him.

"You guys are interrupting my work," he grumbled.

"This won't take long," I said.

"What do you want?"

"We want to talk to you about Chuck Atwood."

His wrinkled face crinkled. "To hell with that guy."

"I don't know if you've been keeping up with current events, but Deputy Atwood is dead."

He smirked. "Good riddance."

My face tensed.

JD's cheeks reddened.

"Deputy Atwood was a friend," I said.

"Well, your friend set me up."

"Is that so?"

"I lost 15 years of my life."

The woman whose groceries Felix sacked had a fearful look on her face. She stood by the debit terminal, card in hand, as the checker scanned items. *Bleep. Bleep. Bleep.* The woman's concerned eyes kept flicking between the three of us as we spoke.

A manager soon approached. "Is there some kind of problem here?"

I flashed my badge. "No, sir. We just need to have a few words with Felix."

"How about you step outside and have this conversation in private?" the manager suggested. He looked at Felix. "Take five."

Felix's face twisted. "I'm gonna miss out on my tip."

At this point in time, I don't think the customer felt too comfortable having Felix follow her out to her car with the groceries.

Felix grumbled but complied. We followed him outside and stepped around to the side of the building.

Felix was livid.

He took the opportunity to have a smoke break. He stuffed a cigarette between his thin lips and struck it up. The cherry glowed as he sucked in a breath, and the smell of fresh tobacco wafted with the breeze.

"You got no right to come here and harass me at my place of work," Felix growled. "I did time for something I didn't do. I just want to live my life and enjoy what time I got left. Look at me. I'm 63 years old. Because of you people, I got nothing. No retirement and a felony conviction on my record. If it weren't for the people at Phoenix House, I'd be on the street and wouldn't have a job. You know what it's like trying to start over at my age?"

"Maybe you should have thought about that before you raped and murdered Darcy Klein?"

His cheeks reddened, and he clenched his jaw tight. His hands balled into fists. "I didn't rape and murder that girl. And I didn't assault the other two girls either. Your buddy, Deputy Atwood, planted the evidence. I got a lawyer, and I'm gonna sue the county."

"Two women ID'd you."

He scoffed. "Of course they did. Deputy Dickwood shoves my picture in front of their face and says *that's the guy. Other witnesses have ID'd him.* And they go along with it. Eyewitness testimony is notoriously inaccurate. And explain this to me... The knife they took off me that was supposedly the murder weapon... How come the blood had traces of a preservative in it?"

That hung there for a moment. EDTA was used as a blood preservative.

"I'll tell you how," Felix continued. "They took that shit from the lab and put it on the knife. Plain as day. And everybody from Atwood on up had a hand in it, including that damn Judge Echols." He shook his head in disgust.

If true, it was a concerning allegation. I was no fan of the judge, either.

"Where were you last night around 10 PM?" I asked.

"I was at Phoenix House."

"They say you weren't there."

He gave me an incredulous look. "Now that's bullshit. Check the logs. I signed in."

"If what you say is true, that's a hell of a reason to kill Deputy Atwood."

"What I said *is* true. And you ain't gonna railroad me again. Find another patsy." He took a last big drag from his cigarette, tossed it aside, and stormed away.

"You know, if he's telling the truth, it means the real perpetrator got away with Darcy's murder and two other assaults," JD said.

"I don't know what to think right now."

We left the grocery store and headed back to Phoenix House. Another check of the register revealed that Felix had, in fact, signed into the facility at 9 PM. The clerk I had spoken to on the phone had made a mistake earlier.

Brenda called as we were leaving. "You ready for this?"

"What have you got?"

"With the use of a spectroscope, I was able to make out the title and edition of that textbook. World History."

"What year?"

"That particular edition was used by the Coconut Key High School in 1988 and 1989," Brenda said.

My brow lifted. "Really?"

"I called the school and talked to a woman in the administration building that has been there since the '80s. She remembered that two girls from the school went missing during that era. Laurie Ferguson and Skyler Locke. Neither one of them ever turned up."

I frowned.

"I made a ton of phone calls and tracked down the dentists for those two girls. Both of them were out of business, but their practices were assumed by new dentists. The files for Laurie Ferguson had long since been discarded."

I frowned again.

"Fortunately, the woman who took over Dr. Rossi's practice maintained all the past records. It seems I caught her in the nick of time. She just hired a document company to shred the old records, and they're taking them next week. She sent the file over for Skyler Locke. After careful examination, I can say with confidence, Skyler Locke is our victim."

"You are amazing," I said. "Have I told you that?"

"I know, and not often enough."

I laughed.

Brenda continued, "Skyler was 16 years old at the time of her disappearance. A junior at the high school. I'll send over her yearbook photo."

"Does she have any family still living on the island?"

"Yes. Her mother's name is Deborah Locke. She lives at 712 Bayshore Drive. I'll text you her phone number."

"You've outdone yourself."

"I got lucky. Now go give the family some closure."

"I will."

I ended the call and gave JD the address for Deborah Locke. A text with Skyler's image buzzed through a moment later. It was heartbreaking to see her gorgeous, smiling face. The brunette had a classic '80s hairdo—parted in the middle, feathered on the sides. She lacked the height to be a fashion model during the era, but she was every bit as pretty.

We zipped across the island. Deborah lived in a nice neighborhood. The two-story French colonial was painted in Heather Gray with white trim. The yard was surrounded by a white picket fence and was full of tall skinny palm trees and green ferns. It looked like a lush tropical paradise. A cobblestone walkway led up to the porch, and there was a silver Lexus SUV in the drive.

We parked at the curb, pushed through the gate, and climbed the steps to the porch. I banged on the door, and not long after a woman's voice filtered through, "Who is it?"

"Coconut County. We'd like to talk to you about Skyler."

The door unlatched and flung open. Deborah's wide eyes greeted us with curiosity. She was 39 in 1989 when her daughter went missing. She'd held her age well. Her short auburn hair was clearly dyed. She kept herself fit and trim, and she had few wrinkles for a woman in her 70s. "Tell me you found her."

I gave her a grim nod.

Her eyes misted with tears. This moment had been over 30 years in the making. "Not the girl you just found in the barrel?"

I nodded. She'd clearly seen the news reports.

Her face quivered, and her eyes misted. She took a deep breath and steadied herself. "Come on in," she said, stepping aside as the pain rolled down her cheeks.

She offered us a seat in the living room. It was a beautiful home, and French doors opened to a patio and a pool. It was clean and cozy, everything in its place. Not cluttered.

Deborah took a seat, and I told her the full story. Sadness twisted on her face. She grabbed a tissue from the coffee table and blotted her eyes as she wept.

"Can you tell us what was going on at the time?"

"Well, let's see... My husband passed away in '86. Tom was a bit of a drinker, sad to say. One night, as he was coming home, he must have passed out on the drive. Swerved off the road and hit a telephone pole. Died instantly. It was a miracle he didn't kill anybody else."

"I'm very sorry."

"It was a difficult time. We went to live with my brother, Paul, until I could get on my feet. We lived there until I got remarried. Somehow, I got pregnant again. Maggie is my miracle baby."

"You live here with your current husband?"

Deborah shook her head. "Victor died two years ago. Stroke." She snapped her fingers. "Had a brain bleed and was dead before he hit the ground. I was devastated at the time, but the more I think about it, the more I believe he got off easy. He didn't have to suffer or linger on as some people do."

"What can you tell me about the day Skyler disappeared?"

She took a moment to recall the era. "I was working at the time. I didn't usually get home until the evenings. Paul worked shifts. Sometimes he was on days, sometimes nights. Anyway, Skyler went to school that day and never came home."

"When did you report her missing?" I asked.

Deborah thought about it for a moment.

"Skyler was always home by dinner. Sometimes, in the afternoon, she'd hang out with friends or do whatever. When she didn't make dinner that night, I started to get worried. I called around to her friends, and they hadn't seen her since school."

"So, she definitely was in school that day?"

"The school confirmed she was in attendance. I called her boyfriend at the time. He hadn't heard from her. I think he came over and went looking for her with Paul at all the usual hangouts. The two of them went out several times over the next few weeks looking for her."

"What was her boyfriend's name?"

"Marshall Noonan."

"What was their relationship like?"

She shrugged. "I guess it was a fairly typical high school relationship. As I recall, Marshall seemed a little possessive."

"Did he get jealous easily?"

"That he did. He wanted her to spend all of her time with him. Skyler was pretty independent and liked her space. I stayed out of her relationships. I figured if I told her what to do, she'd do the opposite."

"Did you two get along?"

"Apart from the usual teenage drama, we had a good relationship. At least, I'd like to think so."

"How did you feel about Marshall?"

"I figured he wouldn't stick around long, and that was fine by me. I really didn't think he was going places. Wasn't the sharpest tool in the shed, if you know what I mean. Good-looking boy. I just kept praying that he didn't knock her up."

JD and I exchanged a glance.

"Do you know for a fact they were engaged in a sexual relationship?"

"It's what hormonal high school kids do. I told her to be careful and use protection. Apart from that, I didn't want too many details."

I hesitated for a moment, trying to determine how to tell Deborah that Skyler was pregnant at the time of her death. When I did, she cried at the loss of a potential grandchild.

"I take it she never mentioned anything?"

Deborah shook her head. "Do you know who the father is?"

"Not at this time," I said.

"With DNA, you should be able to tell, right?"

I nodded. "Yes, ma'am. We'll just need to collect samples from potential fathers."

She lifted a curious eyebrow. "Potential fathers?"

I shrugged. "We have to keep the possibilities open."

Deborah took a deep breath and nodded. "I don't think she was promiscuous, but you never know."

"Did Marshall ever get violent with her?"

"He would get angry. Never in front of me. But Skyler mentioned he would get verbally abusive at times. I told her she didn't need to put up with any of that. I put up with too much of that from her father." She sighed. "Tom, God love him, he was a good man, but when he drank, sometimes it was like a switch had flipped. He could say the meanest things."

"Was he abusive toward Skyler?"

"Physically? No. But they got into a few shouting matches when he'd come home drunk."

"How often was that?"

She shrugged. "More often than I liked."

"What about Skyler's friends?"

"You need to talk to Tiffany McKnight. They were thick as thieves back in the day. Beautiful girl. Bubbly, vivacious. Little bit of a troublemaker. When the two of them got in trouble, it was usually Tiffany's instigating. They were best friends since grade school."

"Do you know if she's still in the area?"

"She is. She's done pretty well for herself too. I see her on that commercial that plays on late-night TV for her real estate company. I'm not sure, but I think she lives over in Stingray Bay."

"I think I know who you're talking about," JD said.

"Is Paul still in town?" I asked.

"He is. He lives a few blocks over on Atlantic Avenue. I can give you the address."

"Please," I said.

"Do you have any idea who did this?" she asked in a desperate tone.

"We'll do everything we can."

"I'd be lying if I said I didn't suspect Marshall. He was obsessed with Skyler. And I think she might have been ready to move on."

18

W e left Deborah's and headed over to Oyster Avenue to grab dinner. Brenda had given me Paul's number and address. I figured we'd talk to him in the morning.

Faye's band, *Lip Bomb,* was playing later, and we had told her we'd show up and offer moral support—not that they needed it. *Lip Bomb* was steadily growing a loyal following.

Jack wanted to eat at *Wetsuit,* and he got no argument for me. There were always plenty of visual delights—waitresses sauntering around in bikini bottoms and tight-fitting neoprene jackets. We took a seat at a high-top table near the bar, and an adorable blonde named Lana took our order.

Crash had never returned my calls, so I figured I would pester him again, just to make sure he was all right. I was starting to get worried about the guy. To my surprise, he picked up the phone when I called. His voice was dreary. "What do you want?"

"Is that any way to talk to your manager?"

He didn't say anything.

"You weren't at band practice the other day. Just want to make sure everything is good with you."

"Oh, yeah, it's just peachy," he said, his voice full of sarcasm.

"I heard about you and Faye."

"I don't want to talk about it."

"Fair enough. But you're part of the band, and you need to come to practice."

"What's the point? I still have my cast on. I can't play. She's doing just fine."

"We're a unit."

"Look, I just can't be around her right now. Okay?" He hesitated, then sighed. "I never should have said anything to her. I shouldn't have told her how I felt. I messed it all up."

I was starting to understand his sharp tone with me. I'd given him the advice to express his feelings to Faye. It didn't work out how he planned. Now he was mad at me. "I can't imagine how being honest with somebody is ever a bad thing."

"It was clearly the wrong thing to do."

I frowned. "I'll keep my mouth shut next time."

Crash said nothing.

"I take it you're not coming to the show tonight," I said.

"No, man. I don't need that kind of torture."

The line was silent for a moment.

"Well, I guess I'll let you get back to whatever you were doing. Call me if you need anything." I ended the call and slipped the phone back into my pocket. I told JD, "I'm staying out of band drama from now on."

"Good luck with that," JD muttered.

We ordered oysters on the half shell and the shrimp and crawfish fondue to start. For an entrée, Jack ordered the blackened Mahi-Mahi with shrimp, spinach, and mushrooms in a tomato cream sauce. I went with the grilled Atlantic salmon, topped with Lafitte sauce and served with jambalaya rice and grilled veggies.

The meal was damn good.

My belly was full, the whiskey was smooth, and there was plenty of eye candy to keep me occupied. My eyes took in the sights and sounds of the restaurant. Smooth music filtered through speakers, and the murmur of conversation filled the air. In a cozy booth against the far wall, I saw something I did not expect.

Ellie was having dinner with a handsome man that looked to be in his mid-20s. It seemed odd since her husband had just passed. Odder still that they were holding hands across the table.

I nudged JD and motioned in their direction. "What do you think that's about?"

He glanced across the restaurant, and a look of surprise washed over his face. "Maybe he's comforting her in her time of need."

"I'll bet he is."

"Far be it from me to judge, but isn't it a little early for Ellie to start dating again?" JD asked.

"By the looks of things, I'm thinking they've been dating for a while."

The couple looked longingly into each other's eyes.

"We probably shouldn't jump to conclusions," JD said, trying to take the high road. "I'm sure there's a perfectly logical explanation. Maybe he's her cousin?"

"They look a little too close for cousins."

"Should we say hello?" JD asked with a devious glint in his eyes.

19

JD flagged down the waitress. He paid the tab and left her a nice tip, slipping a wad of cash into the leather folio. We slugged down the rest of our whiskey, pushed away from the table, and ambled toward Ellie and her new *friend*.

When she saw us approach, her face went pale, and she slipped her hand from the young man's grasp. She looked like a kid that had been caught with her hand in the cookie jar.

"Tyson... JD..." she said, forcing a smile.

"How are you getting along, Ellie?" JD asked.

She swallowed hard and nodded. "Good. I'm trying to get out and get my mind off of things."

There was an awkward pause.

"I'd like you to meet Aaron," she said.

The guy smiled and extended his hand. "How do you do?"

We shook and exchanged pleasantries.

"Aaron is a yoga instructor over at *Mind, Body & Spirit*," Ellie said. "He talked me into getting out after class to clear my head."

"That's very considerate," JD said.

Aaron was a good-looking guy—square jaw, blue eyes, light brown hair. Slender build, but well-defined muscles. He looked like he did well with the ladies.

There was another awkward silence.

"Well, I hate to interrupt," JD said. "But I just wanted to stop by, say hello, and make sure you were doing okay."

Ellie forced another smile. "Thank you."

JD extended his hand to Aaron. "Nice to meet you, Aaron..."

"Pennington. Aaron Pennington."

"You two have a good evening," JD said.

We left the table and strolled away.

"Yoga instructor, huh?" JD muttered under his breath. "I'll bet he's teaching her a few new positions."

We left the restaurant and stepped onto the sidewalk. Oyster Avenue was bustling with activity. Tourists drifted up and down the sidewalks, slipping in and out of bars and restaurants. Music spilled onto the street, and an array of colored lights painted the avenue. The smell of food filled the air. The energy of the night was building.

"Maybe they're just friends," I said, trying to remain objective—*I didn't believe it for a second.*

JD scoffed. "I think we need to look into that little weasel."

We ambled down the block to *Crush*. Faye's band didn't go on until 10:30 PM, which gave us plenty of time to get sufficiently lubricated. It was an alternative bar that rotated themes. Wednesday night was disco. Thursday night was '80s alternative. Friday night was classic rock. Saturday night was hip-hop. Sunday night was smooth jazz. It was a cool little place—dim lighting, deep velour couches. It had a Gothic vibe.

Shadows of Saturn occupied the stage as we arrived. They rocked out an alternative, emo vibe mixed with a little sci-fi psychedelia.

We weaved through the crowd toward the main bar. Faye hung out with her bandmates.

Sadie Savage was the lead singer. She had raven black hair, stunning blue eyes, creamy skin, and a figure that was hard to take your eyes off of. The girl had lungs—she could belt out tones that ranged from gravelly rock 'n' roll to angelic pop falsetto. Lexi Spark was a shredder on guitar. The stunning red-head could work the frets like nobody's business. Katie Thunder pounded out the beat on drums.

Together they formed a quartet that was part punk rock, part '80s New Wave with a dash of '90s Alternative. They had stage presence and all the requisite elements of stardom. They wore short skirts and lacy bras. T-shirts and tank tops cut up and tied tight, exposing flat midriffs. Their makeup was severe and sexy with heavy liner and smoky eyes. They looked like a gang of vampire hunters or a group of girl spies in a B-movie action flick—each with a special power.

Faye greeted us both with a hug. "Thanks for coming!"

"Gotta do our part to support," I said.

"You know the rest of the girls... Sadie, Lexi, Katie."

JD and I smiled and waved. The girls gave a perfunctory smile back. We weren't their favorite people. We'd taken their bass player, and there was an air of suspicion and distrust toward us.

"Are the rest of the guys coming?" Faye asked.

"Dizzy and Styxx should be here soon," I said. "I take it you haven't talked to Crash?"

"I haven't figured out exactly what to say yet. I don't want to make things worse. I need to sort out how I feel. Have you spoken with him? How's he doing?"

"He's upset with me, but he'll live."

"Why you?"

I filled her in on the situation.

Faye rolled her eyes. "That's stupid. You gave him good advice."

It wasn't long before Dizzy and Styxx showed up.

Shadows of Saturn finished their set and loaded their gear offstage. We helped *Lip Bomb* set up their gear, then hung back and enjoyed the show.

The crowd swelled towards the stage, and Sadie belted into the microphone while the band rocked behind her. *Crush* was a small venue, and it was packed full.

The girls put on a damn good show. Afterward, we helped

them break down the gear and load it out. *I think that's the main reason they invited us to see the show.*

We loaded the gear into the back of Sadie's SUV. It was big enough to hold a few amps, speaker cabinets, and guitars. Katie had a system for fitting her entire drum set into the back seat of her car, utilizing the front passenger seat as well.

"You know, you guys aren't half bad," Sadie said in the parking lot as we finished up.

The glow of a mercury vapor light painted her face. Music seeped out from the club, and the stars flickered above.

"At first, I thought you guys were the typical asshole musicians. But you guys are alright."

Dizzy smiled.

"We ought to do a double bill sometime," Sadie suggested.

The guys looked at each other and, after a brief nonverbal conference, gave a nod of approval.

"I'm sure we can arrange a show where you open for us," JD said.

Sadie laughed. "I was thinking maybe you guys could open for us."

JD frowned at her playfully.

Sadie let out an exaggerated sigh. "Fine. I guess we can open for you guys. If you twist my arm."

"Talk to Tyson," JD said. "He's the manager."

"I'm all for the idea," I said. "But... I'm not gonna schedule anything until a certain situation gets worked out." My eyes found Faye.

She huffed. "Is he really gonna be that much of a bitch about it? Is he really at the point where he can't be around me at all?"

I shrugged.

"I told you this was a bad idea," Styxx mumbled to himself.

"Excuse me?" Faye said.

"Nothing."

The two exchanged a look.

"Party on the boat?" Dizzy asked, changing the subject. "What do you say, Tyson?"

I shrugged. "Whatever."

Dizzy turned his attention to the girls. "Ladies?"

The girls exchanged glances, communicating telepathically.

20

"Sure," Sadie said. "Why not? We'll meet you at the boat after we load the gear back into the practice studio."

The girls hopped into their cars and drove away.

We hung out in the parking lot for a moment.

"Do me a favor," I asked. "Keep it tame tonight. Don't do anything that's going to make the current situation worse."

"Relax. It's just a few drinks," Dizzy said with a disarming smile. "Faye's off-limits. We get that. But the others..." he had a mischievous glint in his eyes.

"We'll see you at the boat," Styxx said with a pat on the back and a mischievous grin.

They headed toward their car, and JD and I walked back to Oyster Avenue. We hustled down the sidewalk. We had parked on a side street a few blocks away. We found the Porsche and drove toward the marina. We cruised with the top down, listening to music, the cool night air swirling around.

"We need to improve the ratio," JD said. "We're going back to the boat with four girls, and two of them are off the market."

"Two?"

"The drummer. She dates the singer for that death metal band, *Malice Eternal*. We might have to round up a few more prospects. Just say'n."

The light ahead flashed from yellow to red, and we pulled to a stop at the crosswalk.

Two cars revved their engines, squealed their tires, and launched across the intersection as the light turned green for them. White smoke billowed from wheel wells, and the cars rocketed forward. The Mustang got the jump off the line, but the Corvette quickly made up ground.

The rip of exhaust echoed through the night air.

At 2nd gear, the driver of the Corvette lost control.

The car spun out and careened across the oncoming lanes of traffic, narrowly missing a vehicle. Rubber tracks stained the asphalt. The Corvette plowed into a telephone pole on the corner, and the hood cracked and crumbled, splintering fiberglass. The brand-new pumpkin orange sports car was a mess.

As soon as the light turned green for us, JD banked a hard left and sped to the crash site a block away.

The Mustang was long gone.

The driver of the Corvette tried to get the car started but couldn't get the engine to turn over. It was a prior model with a front engine before they switched to a mid-engine design.

I hopped out of the Porsche and stormed toward the driver's side of the Corvette. With my weapon drawn, and my badge displayed, I shouted, "Coconut County! Out of the car, now!"

The kid kept trying to get the car started, but it wouldn't turn over. The airbags had deployed, and the kid was dazed.

"Out of the vehicle. Now!"

I recognized him. He was Nick Hartsell's kid, Cameron.

I yanked open the driver's door, and grabbed hold of his shirt collar, and pulled him out of the vehicle. He staggered and stumbled to the ground, clearly intoxicated.

JD pounced on him and slapped the cuffs around his wrists.

His girlfriend sobbed, blood trickling from her nose. Her face was scuffed and raw.

An airbag deploys like a cannon. They may save your life, but they can create injuries of their own—abrasions, broken bones, ocular damage.

I dialed 911 and attended to the girl.

The EMTs arrived a few minutes later. It wasn't long before several patrol cars were on the scene. Flashing lights bathed the area.

We took pictures of the scene, and EMTs treated Cameron and his girlfriend. A crowd had gathered around. Traffic ground to a halt, and deputies managed the chaos.

In an abundance of caution, Cameron and his girlfriend were transferred to the ER where they'd receive x-rays and CT scans to make sure there was no brain trauma or internal bleeding. Afterward, Cameron would be booked on DUI, reckless driving, and a host of other charges.

It was a damn shame the sleek sports car was mangled. But it didn't mean anything to Cameron. He didn't pay for it. It was a car from his father's dealership. It had dealer plates. I'm sure Nick wouldn't be too happy about the situation.

A wrecker towed the vehicle away, and a cleanup crew swept up bits of fiberglass and plastic from the roadway. It took about an hour to sort out. I called the guys to tell them there would be no after-party on the boat tonight. It was probably for the best, anyway. I'm sure Crash wouldn't have been too thrilled about Faye partying with us on the boat, even if they were broken up.

We wrapped up at the scene and headed to the station to fill out after-action reports. Not exactly how I wanted to spend the latter part of the evening. It was almost 2 AM by the time JD dropped me off at the marina. I told him I'd catch up with him in the morning and ambled down the dock toward the *Avventura*.

The rumble of the Porsche's engine filled the air as he peeled out of the parking lot and raced home.

I took Buddy for a walk, then settled in for bed.

In the morning, I called Denise and asked her to find out as much information as she could about Aaron Pennington. "He's a yoga instructor at *Mind, Body & Spirit*."

"Do you really think Ellie's having an affair with him?"

"Sure looked like it last night," I said. "I'll reserve judgment until I know more."

"Ballistics came back. Chuck was shot with a 9mm. Probably some type of submachine gun, judging by the amount of bullets and the statements given by Justin and his girlfriend, Kennedy."

"Thanks. Keep me posted."

"I will."

I hung up and called JD. He swung by the marina 15 minutes later and picked me up. We headed over to Paul Locke's house at 2113 Atlantic Avenue. He lived in a pastel yellow home with a cobblestone drive and walkway. There were a few palm trees out front, and the flower beds were set off with stone trim. A silver compact SUV was parked out front. The one-story home had vaulted ceilings and transom windows. It looked like it had been recently renovated. It was small but nice. Extremely well maintained.

We parked out front and strolled to the front door. Paul was retired, so I hoped we'd catch him at home. I banged on the door and waited.

21

Through the frosted glass, I saw somebody approach the front door. Paul pulled it open, and I flashed our credentials and made introductions.

Paul was in his mid-70s. He was bald on top and had stark white hair on the sides that was close-cropped. He had a round face and a rounder torso. His plump cheeks sagged, giving him deep laugh lines. His chin gave way to a saggy neck. He had bushy eyebrows and deep-set eyes that were probably vibrant blue at one point but were more of a hazel-grayish color now.

Paul had a little bit of stubble, having skipped the morning shave. The man had a nice complexion but was a little red in the cheeks. There was a bulbous growth in the corner of his nose that was hard not to notice. "I spoke with Deborah. I figured you'd be stopping by at some point."

I expressed our condolences, and Paul invited us in.

There was a study to the left of the foyer with a desk and bookshelves that were full of leather-bound tomes.

Paul escorted us into the living room, hobbling behind us. "I'm a little slow these days. This hip threw craps on me."

He offered us a seat.

"Nice place you've got here."

"Thank you."

"Is this the home you were living in at the time of Skyler's disappearance?" I asked.

Paul nodded. "Can I get you boys anything to drink? Water? Soda? Beer?"

I smiled. "Thank you, but no."

He took a seat and winced as he gently lowered himself into the recliner. "Deborah gave me all the gory details." Paul shook his head. "It's just horrible. I sure hope Skyler didn't suffer." He sighed and his eyes misted. "I guess it's just random chance you found her. Funny how that works out. I always hoped we'd learn the truth, but I thought I'd probably go to my grave without knowing. It's been eating away at me all these years."

"Can you walk me through the day she disappeared?"

"Well, I was off work that day. Skyler never came home from school, which wasn't entirely unusual. You know how kids are. They get sidetracked with their friends sometimes."

"Where were you working?"

"In those days, I owned my own truck and was driving drop and hooks at night, mostly."

He told us the same story Deborah did.

"When Skyler hadn't shown up by 9 o'clock, Deborah was in a panic. She called all of Skyler's friends, and nobody had seen her since school. She called that boyfriend of hers, Marshall. He came over to the house that night, and I remember he and I went driving around looking for Skyler. He took me to all the hangouts the kids frequented in those times. We didn't find hide nor hair of her. We must have gone out looking for her every night for the next couple of weeks."

"What are your thoughts about Marshall Noonan?" I asked.

Paul shrugged. "I think he was an okay kid. He had his issues. He got in a little trouble here and there. But hell, we all did at that age. I didn't ever see their relationship as anything long-term for Skyler."

"You think he could have had some involvement in her disappearance? Deborah mentioned he was the jealous type and didn't seem to control his anger well."

"I know Deborah never much cared for Marshall. But I spent a lot of time with that kid looking for Skyler. If he was faking it, he was a damn good actor 'cause he was beside himself. Utterly distraught."

"What about Skyler's friend Tiffany McKnight?"

His brow lifted, and a grin tugged his lips. "Whew! She was a looker. Let me tell you. I'm surprised she didn't go on to become a model or a beauty queen or something like that. That girl developed fast if you know what I mean. I see her every now and then on the TV commercials. Looks like she's still got it."

"How long did Skyler live here?"

Paul thought for a moment. "Oh, let me see. I think she was 12 or 13 when her dad died. They came to live here for three years or so until she disappeared. I think her mother stayed around another year before she met Victor. I'm kinda hazy on the timeline. It was a long time ago."

"Did Skyler ever talk to you about anything that was bothering her?"

"What do you mean?"

"Problems she was having with other people. Anybody who might have wanted to hurt her?"

"You think this was somebody she knew?"

I shrugged. "It usually is."

"I always figured she was picked up by some random serial killer. Or maybe some boys lured her into a trap and killed her. I don't want to think about what could have been done to her."

"How was your relationship with her?"

"I think it was good. I mean, kids can be difficult at that age. They start to rebel. I let her mother discipline her, for the most part. Every now and then, I had to lay down the law. It was my home, after all." He sighed. "But she was a good kid. It's a damn shame. She had so much potential."

He wiped his eyes as they misted.

"If there's anything else you can remember about that time..."

"If you really want to know what was going on with her, talk to Tiffany. I'm sure Skyler told her everything."

"She's on our list."

"I'm sure glad you boys are on top of this. Maybe after all these years, Skyler can get some peace."

"I hope so," I said.

I handed him my card. "If you think of anything else…"

He pushed off the armrests to stand.

"Don't get up," I said. "We'll show ourselves out."

Paul got up anyway and showed us to the door. We strolled the walkway to the Porsche, and Paul watched from the doorway.

We climbed in, and JD cranked up the engine.

Paul smiled and waved as we drove away.

I called Tiffany McKnight. She was showing a house in the *Platinum Dunes Estates*. She said we could stop by and talk after she finished with her client. She'd heard about it on the news and had already spoken with Deborah Locke.

We drove over to the posh neighborhood that was filled with McMansions, oversize SUVs, and exotic sports cars. Lawn crews attended to the landscaping, and a leaf blower buzzed a few doors down from the house Tiffany was showing.

I don't want to say all the homes in the Platinum Dunes Estates looked the same, but they all had a similar design aesthetic and common themes. For several million dollars, you too could live in the lap of luxury.

We pulled to the curb in front of the sprawling estate. There were two cars in the circular driveway. The white Lexus SUV belonging to Tiffany had a magnetic sign with her company logo stuck to the door. Her client drove a black jaguar convertible.

We hopped out of the Porsche and walked up to the front door. JD pushed it open, and we stepped into the foyer. "Hello? Is anybody home?"

His voice echoed off the high walls and vaulted ceilings.

"Deputy Wild?" a voice called from the living room.

"Yes. I'm with Deputy Donovan."

"Make yourself at home. Feel free to look around. I'll be with you shortly."

We took the time to wander around, scoping out the luxury home. It was fully staged with contemporary art on the walls and sleek modern furniture. There was travertine tile on the floor. A spiral staircase led up to the second story.

JD and I climbed the steps and scoped out the bedrooms. There were four upstairs in total, plus a living area with a flatscreen display, couch, and game console—a place the kids could make a racket and not disturb the adults downstairs. There was a terrace that overlooked the patio and the pool. Beyond that, the canal was home to yachts, sport boats, and bluewater sailboats. The walls were painted with the standard-issue light beige, and the upstairs was covered with sand-colored carpeting.

It was a nice home, no doubt about it.

We stayed out of the way until Tiffany finished with her client. Their voices echoed as they stepped into the foyer. The two women said their goodbyes as Tiffany escorted her client to the door. As soon as the client was gone, Tiffany congratulated herself, "Yes!"

I figured that was our cue, and we made our way downstairs.

"I take it things went well?"

"I think it's a done deal. I'll fax over the paperwork when I get back to the office."

Tiffany was in her early 50s, but she looked closer to 43. She had a little work done here and there, but she'd taken care of herself rather well over the years. She was dressed in a pastel blue blazer and skirt with a cream blouse. She wore cream spike-heeled shoes and had a large sparkling diamond on her finger and a few dangling from her ears. The standard-issue, business professional pearl necklace was draped around her collar bones.

As we hit the first-floor landing, we made formal introductions.

"Thanks for taking the time to speak with us," I said.

"Thanks for working on this case. I'd given up hope. I thought Skyler would never be found. She was my best friend. And after all these years, I still couldn't get her out of my head. Every now and then, I would see her in my dreams. She was just as she always was, and we'd have a random conversation. When I woke, I could never remember what we talked about. I kept thinking that maybe the answer was in our conversations. I'd always tried to write them down when I woke, but it never seemed to make any sense. Skyler popped into my head just the other day. Then I saw the story on the news. Crazy."

"When was the last time you saw Skyler?" I asked.

"The day she went missing. She was in school that day. I had detention, imagine that, and had to stay after. I told her we'd catch up in the afternoon, maybe go to the mall. But I didn't hear from her. This was before cell phones. I remember I called the house, and she wasn't there."

"Did you talk to Paul?"

Her face crinkled. "You know, I don't remember if I got the answering machine or if I talked to Paul. I've killed some brain cells since then. Margaritas are my guilty pleasure. Anyway, I figured Skyler blew me off and was hanging out with Marshall. Then her mom called in a panic that evening."

"Tell me about Marshall."

"Total loser. Have you talked to him yet?"

I shook my head.

"Life sure hasn't been kind to him. Didn't age well," she muttered. "But he sure was cute back in the day."

"What was their relationship like?"

"He was kind of a dick. You know, the jealous, insecure type. He always wanted to know where she was, who she was with, what she was doing."

"Do you know if he ever got abusive with her?"

She cringed. "They were always getting in fights about something. She told me he hit her once. Could have been more than that, who knows? I told her she was crazy to stick around. He was a loser. He wasn't going anywhere. And boy, did I call that one right."

"You think he could have had anything to do with her disap-pearance?"

She looked at me like it was a dumb question. "He was the first person I blamed. I could totally see him getting jealous. They get into a fight, and things get out of control. Next thing you know, she's dead, and he's gotta get rid of the body."

"We talked to Paul. He said they searched for Skyler together."

"Of course they did. What else was Marshall gonna do? All eyes were on him at the time. He put on a good show. Acted devastated. Searched everywhere. He put up flyers all over town. I remember the cops questioned him at the time, but they never got anything on him. Hell, I think he's been in and out of jail a few times on domestic assault. I wouldn't be surprised if he killed more people too." She sighed. "Some people seem to get away with everything."

"Did Skyler tell you that she was pregnant?"

"No. She never said anything to me about it. I was shocked when Deborah told me."

"You and Skyler were close, right?"

"Extremely. I didn't think we kept secrets from each other. Maybe she didn't know she was pregnant?"

"Was she seeing anyone else besides Marshall?"

Tiffany hesitated. "Well, sort of."

"Sort of?"

"She told me she hooked up with this married guy a couple of times."

JD and I exchanged a glance.

"He was obviously older."

"Like how older?"

"I think he was like 40," she muttered.

I lifted a surprised brow. "Really? Do you know who?"

"She never told me his name." Tiffany frowned. "We thought it was so cool at the time. Sophisticated. Worldly. It's just creepy now. Looking back on it, I guess there were a few things she kept from me." She sighed. "I like to think that I'm a vault, but I do run my mouth a little bit when I get tipsy."

She cringed.

"Were you getting tipsy a lot when you were 16?"

Tiffany gave me another look like it was a dumb question. "Don't act like you two never got in trouble when you were kids. We were always getting into some kind of mischief. We'd sneak vodka from Paul's wet bar and replace it with water. It was easy to find somebody to buy a six-pack of beer or something from the liquor store. Especially in that day and age. Hell, back then, we'd just get all dolled up, put on sunglasses, and buy it ourselves sometimes." She laughed at the memory. "We'd wear low-cut tops and push the girls together, and the clerks would never card us. My God! The cheap wine we used to drink. And we thought it was good, too." She smiled and shook her head, thinking about the good old days.

"Was there anybody else that she was involved with at the time? Guys that may have had a crush on her?"

Her face sparked with a realization. "Oh, yeah. Tommy Halford. He had such a crush on her. He was this dweeby little guy. No social skills. Just weird. He followed her around at school. He would stare endlessly, then just turn around and shuffle away when she looked at him." She took a deep breath and looked at the ceiling while she thought. "I can't prove it, but I swear there was one time when Skyler was spending the night at my house... I could have sworn I saw somebody peeping in through the window while we were getting changed. I'm pretty sure it was Tommy Halford." She laughed. "I'm sure he enjoyed the show."

She looked at her watch. "Listen, I gotta run to my next appointment. But I'm happy to talk to you guys anytime. And if I remember anything else, I'll give you a call." A solemn frown tugged her face. "I really hope you find out who did this. And if it's that Marshall Noonan creep, you nail his ass to the wall, you got me?"

"I gotcha."

She showed us out, locked up, and clicked her key fob. The lights flashed on her SUV. She called to us as we walked toward the Porsche. "The next time you need to sell your home, give me a call."

I smiled and waved as I climbed into the Porsche. Jack pulled away from the curb, and I called Denise. "Tell me everything you know about Marshall Noonan."

23

Nothing Denise told me was surprising. Marshall Noonan had a list of felonies and misdemeanors a mile long. He'd been in and out of jail multiple times, and the odds were good he'd be heading back there soon. Assault, battery, domestic abuse, DUI, possession of a controlled substance, and a host of other petty charges. He lived with his girlfriend, Heather Wallace, in Sunset Park.

We pulled into the parking lot and cruised through the rows of mobile homes. JD was a little leery about driving the Porsche into the community. The car always left with an extra dent or scratch.

Some of the trailers were well maintained and trimmed with latticework around the base and colorful gardens of flowers. Others were rusted out and overgrown with weeds.

A couple of kids were tossing a baseball around the lot, and Jack went out of his way to avoid them. He'd already had a few run-ins with an errant football the last time we were here.

We parked on the opposite end of the parking lot from the potential window breakers and walked toward Noonan's trailer. It was actually his girlfriend's trailer. JD clicked the alarm, and the lights on the Porsche flashed.

We climbed the wooden steps to the porch and banged on the door. The windows rattled, and JD shouted, "Coconut County!"

There was some commotion inside, and muffled voices seeped out.

Footsteps rumbled toward the door.

Marshall shouted. "What do you want?"

"We just have a few questions?"

"You got a warrant?"

"This is just a friendly conversation."

"The hell it is. Come back with a warrant."

"I get suspicious when I have to get warrants. It would be a lot easier if you just talked to us."

"What the hell did you do now?" Heather growled.

"I ain't done nothing," Noonan replied.

"If you ain't done nothing, open the door." Heather's footsteps pattered across the trailer, the handle rattled, and much to Marshall's dismay, she swung open the door. A rush of air, stale with cigarette smoke, smacked us in the face.

Heather smiled at us. "You'll have to excuse his manners."

Marshall glared at her, anger swelling on his face.

Heather had long blonde hair curled on the ends. Short bangs fell into her eyes that were rimmed with blue eyeliner. She wore a yellow skirt and had a two-tier muffin top that drooped over her waistline.

She spun around, marched back to the couch, and plopped down to resume watching her show.

Noonan's angry gaze followed her. Then he stared at us with concerned eyes. He looked us up and down as I flashed my badge.

"I didn't do nothing," Marshall said again.

"I haven't even mentioned why we're here," I said.

"Anytime a cop shows up at my door, it can't be good."

"I take it you don't watch the news or read the paper?"

Marshall scowled. "Hell no. It's all noise."

Marshall Noonan was in his early 50s, and he hadn't held up too well. He was a thin, wiry guy. His once strong features had turned into drawn cheeks, hard lines, a crinkled brow, and a receding hairline. His brown hair was short and messy. It looked like it hadn't been washed in a day or two. He had a goatee that was graying, and there was a sadness about his eyes. He looked older than he should have, and the years of bad luck and poor decisions had taken a toll on his face, constantly tensed with anger. He was mad at the system and lived in a state of perpetual discontent.

I told him that we had discovered Skyler Locke's body submerged in a barrel of chemicals.

His brow lifted with surprise. "No shit? No wonder we never found her." He hung his head and frowned. "That's just a damn shame. A tragedy, really. She was such a beautiful girl. I was so in love with her back then."

Noonan's girlfriend scoffed at that one. "Sounds like she got off easy then."

"Shut up," Noonan barked.

It was clear Heather was over his shit.

"Did you love her enough to beat her?" I asked.

Noonan's face crinkled with anger. "What are you talking about?"

"You were never verbally and physically abusive with Skyler?"

His scowl persisted. "Where'd you hear that nonsense? Tiffany? Bitch!" He huffed. "She always did think she was above everyone else. I see her every now and then on those goddamn commercials. I ran into her one time at a convenience store, and she was as rude as could be. All that money she's got doesn't make her better than me." He paused for a moment. "She can say whatever she wants, but I loved Skyler with all my heart."

Heather scoffed again.

"I searched for her night and day when she first went missing," Noonan continued.

"Where did you look?"

"All the usual places. At that time, we had hangouts on the island, and sometimes we'd go out to Angelfish or

Barracuda or Crystal Key. But that was usually weekend stuff."

"You searched with Paul, right?"

"As I recall," Marshall said, nodding. "There were a couple weeks where we were going out every day. We got to the point where we had looked everywhere on the island that we could think of. Took his boat out looking too, but never thought to look for a barrel under the water."

"Did you have access to a boat at that time?" I asked.

"My dad had a 23-foot center-console. He let me borrow it from time to time." His face tightened. "Don't think I don't know where you're going with this. I didn't have nothing to do with Skyler's disappearance. So, you guys need to get that out of your head right now."

"Were you having any problems or disagreements with Skyler?"

He shrugged. "I mean, we used to fight a lot. But that's how you know you really love someone. Only somebody you really care about can piss you off that way."

"That's an interesting viewpoint," I said.

"That's passion," he said.

Heather scoffed again.

"You better keep your mouth shut, or I'm gonna show you real passion," Marshall said in a sharp tone.

Noonan wasn't the brightest bulb in the box, making a veiled threat to his girlfriend in the presence of police officers.

"So, you never got physical with Skyler?" I asked, my voice thick with sarcasm.

"What do you mean, physical? I mean, we got *physical* alright," he said with a sly grin. "We used to fuck like rabbits."

"I bet she enjoyed that," Heather said flatly.

Noonan's face tensed, and he glared at her again.

"You never got *passionate* with your fists?" I asked.

Noonan's angry eyes burned into me. "I told you. I never hit her."

He looked over his shoulder at Heather as a warning to keep her mouth shut.

She kept watching the TV and took a drag from her cigarette.

"Tell me about Skyler's uncle," I said.

"We got along. Like I said, we searched the high heavens for her. I never met Skyler's dad. Paul was the closest thing to a father she had. We'd drink a beer together on occasion. Even got high once."

"Did Skyler ever mention anything about being pregnant?"

Noonan's brow lifted. "She was pregnant?"

I nodded.

"Do you guys know who the father is?"

"We'd sure like to find out."

He thought about it for a moment. "I guess it *is* possible. We didn't always use protection."

"Do you know if she was seeing anyone else at the time?"

His face reddened. "I was all she needed."

Heather scoffed again.

Noonan shot her another glare.

"Are you willing to give us a DNA sample?" I asked.

Marshall hesitated for a moment. "I'll have to decline, gentlemen."

"What's the harm in giving a sample?"

"I ain't giving you guys shit without a court order. You're barking up the wrong tree. You need to be looking at that dweeb Tommy Halford. That's the kind of guy that would kill her and stuff her in a barrel."

"Why do you say that?"

"That little geek couldn't get laid in a whore house. He was always following Skyler around. I had to beat his ass one day."

"And how did that work out?"

"Obviously not too well, or she wouldn't have ended up in a barrel."

We heard a bump followed by a crunch and the sound of breaking glass. A car alarm screeched across the parking lot. An engine roared, and tires squealed.

We glanced to the parking lot as a lapis green hunk of shit pulled out and raced away.

JD's face soured.

24

"Son-of-a-bitch!" JD grumbled, staring at the mangled front end of his Porsche.

The green heap of junk backed into it, dented the hood, busted the headlight, and cracked the front bumper cover. Not a cheap fix by any stretch of the imagination.

"Did you get the plates of that car?"

I shook my head. I asked Noonan if he knew who owned the car.

He just shrugged, and an amused grin curled his weathered face. "Can't help you." He paused. "Well, gentlemen, I enjoyed the conversation." It was clear he didn't. "Hope you find Skyler's killer."

"We'll be in touch," I said as he closed the door.

JD's face was red, and the veins in his temples pulsed.

"You want to wait for the driver to come back?"

"I got a better idea." JD marched to the nearest mobile home and banged on the door.

Nobody answered so Jack moved on to the next. Another knock, and no answer.

He moved to a third trailer and hammered a heavy fist, repeatedly knocking.

"I'm coming, I'm coming," a creaky old voice replied.

JD flashed his badge when the annoyed old lady pulled open the door. "You know who drives a beat to shit dark green import with Bondo on the quarter-panels?"

"That eye-sore? That's Darby's car. Lives with RayLynn." She pointed across the parking lot to another trailer. "What's he done now?"

"Bastard ran into my car. You know his last name?"

"Nope. Don't know what RayLynn sees in him. Then again, she ain't no prize, neither."

He thanked the woman and shuffled down the steps. We marched across the lot to RayLynn's trailer, climbed the steps, and knocked on the door.

RayLynn pulled open the door a moment later. She was a rail-thin red-head in her mid 40s with a tanned face wrinkled like shoe leather. Pretty blue eyes. Missing a few teeth.

JD flashed his badge.

RayLynn groaned. "If this is about that bitch, Mary Lou, she swung first. It was self-defense."

JD and I exchanged a quick glance.

"No," JD said. "It's not about Mary Lou. It's about Darby and that green hunk of shit he drives."

"What about him?"

"He live here?"

"He ain't got a place of his own."

"Know where he went?"

"To get some beer and more cigarettes. What's he done now?"

"What store?"

"How the hell should I know?"

"What's Darby's last name?"

"Glick."

"Thanks," JD said, then plunged down the steps.

"What's this about?" she shouted after us.

JD ignored her and called the Sheriff's Department. He told dispatch to put a BOLO out for Darby Glick and his green trash heap for felony hit and run. He marched back to the parking lot and surveyed the damage again. He frowned and shook his head. Jack was having terrible luck with the car.

We waited around for a while, but Darby didn't show. I had a sneaking suspicion that RayLynn called and tipped him off.

We headed back to the station, and JD filled out a report. Afterward, we caught up with Denise.

"You're going to find this interesting," she said. "I dug into your yoga instructor friend."

"He ain't my friend," JD said.

"His real name isn't Aaron Pennington."

JD and I both lifted a surprised brow.

"Who is he?" I asked.

"I went to the yoga website, grabbed his picture from their instructors' page, then ran it through the facial recognition database. His real name is Aaron Patterson. And, he was a person of interest in another murder."

Denise had our full attention.

"Apparently, he was having an affair with a married woman in Pineapple Bay. Her husband was shot during a mugging, and the woman collected a $1 million insurance policy. I talked to Deputy Hooper, who worked the case. He said they looked into Aaron, but they couldn't make anything stick. The woman's name was Vanessa Redman, and her husband was Ray. Deputy Hooper said that her relationship with Aaron didn't last long after Ray's death. As soon as Vanessa got the insurance money, Aaron talked her into investing in a *startup* that went bust."

"Sounds like Aaron might be a con man," I said.

"Ellie is set to inherit a sizable sum," Denise said. "Factor in her survivor pension, the 401K, the basic life insurance, plus the supplemental policy Chuck bought, Ellie will be well taken care of."

"And I'll bet Aaron has his eye on all of that," JD said.

"So, Aaron staged Ray's death to look like a mugging gone wrong," I said.

"That's the theory. Hooper thinks Aaron was working with an accomplice. I told him I'd keep him posted about the situation here. And before you ask, I double-checked ballistics. There is no connection between the Ray Redman murder and Chuck."

"I think Ellie needs to know who she's dealing with," I said.

"I hate to say it, but she may be in on it," Denise replied.

I frowned. I didn't want to think that way about Ellie. "You got the number for Vanessa Redman handy? I think we need to have a little talk."

"I sure do. Also, Brenda tracked down the shipping info of that barrel Skyler was found in. The sodium hydroxide was shipped to a soap company here in town that went out of business in the '90s. It was owned by Randy Murdoch at the time, then later sold. The warehouse they operated in is now vacant. Randy still lives here in town. I'll send you his address along with Vanessa's contact information. Randy Murdock is close to 80 now."

I looked at JD. Randy could be our *married man.* He was the right age.

We left the station and grabbed a bite to eat at *Gators* before heading over to the *Breakwater Estates* to speak with Randy Murdoch. It was a nice community filled with French Colonial houses in pastel colors with plenty of palm trees and picket fences. It wasn't *Stingray Bay,* but it was nice.

On the drive over, I called Vanessa Redman.

25

Vanessa didn't want anything to do with me. All I could get out of her were a few unsavory words about Aaron before she hung up. Hell, if I conspired to have my significant other murdered, I wouldn't want to talk to a deputy either.

Randy Murdoch lived in a villa with a Spanish tile roof. A 6-foot wall surrounded the property, and there were wrought-iron gates at the pedestrian entrance and driveway.

A carport kept the sun off a black Mercedes. Palm trees and other foliage shrouded the house. He'd clearly done well for himself in the soap business. The two-story home had a pool out back and was a little oasis just two blocks from the beach.

We parked at the curb, pushed through the wrought-iron gate into the courtyard, and climbed the steps to the front porch. I rang the bell and waited for a response.

Mrs. Murdoch peered through the distorted privacy glass in the door and asked, "Who is it?"

I flashed my badge. "Coconut County. Is Randy available?"

She pulled open the door and eyed us with suspicion. "He's not here right now. He's at the country club, playing golf. Might I ask what this is in reference to?"

She was a frail woman, close to 80, with a slight hunch to her back. She had a narrow face, bushy grey hair, and thick glasses. Her skin hung on her bones, spotted with age.

I didn't want to give away everything just yet. "We think your husband might be able to help us solve a cold case."

That seemed to pique her interest.

I pulled out my phone and showed her a picture of Skyler from the yearbook. "Do you happen to recognize this girl?"

She studied the image, looking down her nose through her multi-focal glasses at the image. "I can't say that I do."

The remote gate opened, and a white Mercedes drove inside the compound.

"That's Randy now," Mrs. Murdoch said.

Randy parked the car, killed the engine, and climbed out. He gazed at us with curiosity. He walked around the trunk and ambled down the path toward the main steps.

"Randy, these gentlemen are here from Coconut County. They want to talk to you." She had an uneasy tone in her voice.

Randy grabbed hold of the handrail and climbed the steps to the porch. He was pretty spry for a man of his *experience*.

We made introductions and shook hands.

"What seems to be the trouble?"

"No trouble," I said. "As I was telling your wife, we're just trying to wrap up an old cold case."

Randy smiled. "Anything I can do to help."

I showed him Skyler's picture. He squinted and studied through multi-focals of his own. I watched his face carefully for any hint of a reaction or recognition. He kept a stone face. "Nope. Don't know her. Who is she?"

"Skyler Locke?"

A wave of recognition washed over his face. "That's the girl they found in the barrel, right?" He looked at the picture again. "Now she looks familiar. I just saw that on the news the other day. But I didn't have my glasses on when they showed it on the screen. It never ceases to amaze me what people are capable of."

"That's what brings us here. We tracked that barrel to the manufacturer, then to the chemical company, and onto its final destination."

"I'm not sure I follow."

"That barrel was shipped to your facility in March 1988."

Randy lifted a surprised brow. "Really? If you say so. We used plenty of chemicals back in those days, and sodium hydroxide was one of them."

I didn't mention that the barrel contained sodium hydroxide, but that information could have easily been obtained from the newspaper or TV.

"Do you recall anything about that time?" I asked.

He chuckled. "That was a long time ago, son. I can't seem to remember what I had for breakfast, and you want me to remember the specifics of a barrel of chemicals we got over 30 years ago?"

"I understand, but anything you can remember would be helpful."

"We got a lot of chemicals at that time. Part of the manufacturing process. We weren't regulated as highly back then, so a lot of those barrels ended up in all kinds of places. I paid a guy at the time to haul junk off the lot, and we sold a lot of those barrels to the public. Hell, we practically gave them away. At that point in time, people would wash them out and convert them to barbecue grills, use them as trash cans or rain catches. Hell, I even knew one guy who made a pontoon boat out of those damn things. They'll float if they're water-tight. Just because that barrel was shipped to my facility doesn't mean what you think it means."

"True. But it could be somebody associated with your company. How many employees did you have at the time?"

"Oh, I don't know. Maybe a dozen."

"Do you have any employment records?"

Randy shook his head. "I got rid of that stuff a long time ago when I sold the company."

"Can you remember any names?"

"Let me see... Kenneth was the operations manager. There was George, Edward, Gary, Sam..." He thought for another moment. "I hired kids for the summer. Some of their names escape me. There was one kid named Sean. I believe a kid named Truman worked for me for a while. Marshall worked for me quite a bit. He was part-time during the school year and full time during summers."

"Marshall Noonan?" I asked.

"Yeah, that's his name."

I described Marshall's appearance just to be certain.

"Yeah, that's him."

I showed him Skyler's picture again. "She was Marshall's girlfriend at the time. Are you sure you never met her?"

Randy shrugged. "It's hard to say. I recall he did bring someone around once or twice. He introduced her as his girlfriend. But I honestly can't say if this young lady in the picture is the same person."

"How would you describe Marshall's personality?"

"Typical teenager. As I recall, he worked hard and showed up on time. You think he had something to do with this?"

"Could be."

Randy frowned and shook his head. "I hope you sort this out. It's a terrible tragedy."

"Did you know Skyler was pregnant at the time?" I studied his face for a reaction.

"They may have mentioned it on the news. I don't recall Marshall saying anything about it at the time."

He seemed unfazed. If Randy *was* the married man, I didn't figure he'd admit to the affair in front of his wife.

I gave him my card. "Thank you. You've been extremely helpful. We may be in contact with more questions."

"I'm happy to help."

We left Randy's estate and headed back to Sunset Park, hoping to catch up with Marshall. Seems like he had some explaining to do.

26

J D kept his eyes peeled for the green beater as we returned to Sunset Park. There was no sign of the vehicle.

Jack found a place to park that gave him at least one space between other cars. We hopped out and hustled across the lot to the trailer that Heather Wallace rented. We climbed the steps and banged on the door, rattling the windows again.

Heather stomped to the door and pulled it open. A lit cigarette dangled from her thin lips. "He ain't here."

"Where is he?"

"He took my car to get beer." She took a drag from her cigarette and blew the smoke up toward the ceiling. The place reeked of it. "So what's the story? Did he kill the girl? Should I be concerned?"

"Has Marshall ever gotten violent with you?" I asked.

She scoffed. "Yeah, but he found out real quick I hit back. He tried that shit once, and I beat his ass. I ain't like his past girlfriends."

She looked over our shoulder at the maroon Toyoma that pulled into the parking lot. "That's him now."

We looked at the car, and Marshall looked at us. His eyes widened, and he punched it. The tires did their best imitation of a squeal. More like a chirp. The little four-banger engine rumbled, and the exhaust rattled as he raced through the parking lot.

JD and I plummeted down the steps, sprinted across the parking lot, and hopped into the Porsche. Just as we did, Darby's green trash can pulled into the lot.

JD gave a glance in Darby's direction, then decided to go after Marshall instead.

JD's foot mashed the pedal, and we raced out of the lot and onto the road. He floored it, and the flat-six howled. The tachometer redlined, and the wind swirled around the cabin. Exhaust rumbled.

Marshall banked a hard right, screeching around the corner, the small tires barely holding traction.

I called dispatch and told them we were in pursuit. I gave a description of the car and plate number.

We kept after Marshall as he raced down the road, doing 70 miles an hour in a 35 zone. We caught up to him in no time, but he blasted through a red light.

Cars screeched, and horns honked as he careened through the intersection.

Marshall took a hard left at the next corner, and the back end swung wide, tires squealing. He managed to straighten out the vehicle and plow down the neighborhood street.

I held on as JD followed. The Porsche cornered like it was on rails.

Marshall barreled down the narrow street. There were cars parked on either side, and palm trees shrouded the lane. There was a stop sign ahead, and a guy in a white truck pulled out.

Noonan was going too fast to do anything about it. He slammed on the brakes, and tires squealed billowing white smoke. Marshall twisted the wheel to avoid the truck and plowed onto the shoulder, knocking over the stop sign, smashing into a tree.

The airbags deployed, the hood crumpled and crinkled, the grill shattered, and bits of plastic and glass from the head-lights scattered the area. Steam billowed from under the buckled hood, the radiator cracked.

We pulled behind the vehicle, and I hopped out with my weapon drawn. I advanced toward the driver's side and shouted, "Out of the car! Now!"

The airbag had punched him in the face, and he looked dazed and pissed off. He raised his hands, kicked open the door, and staggered out.

"On the ground! Now!"

He complied and put his hands behind his head, his face against the hot asphalt that had been baked by the sun all morning.

JD slapped the cuffs around his wrists and yanked him to his feet.

I holstered my weapon, called dispatch, and gave them our location.

"Why did you run?" I asked.

"Why did you chase me?"

"Guilty people run," I said.

"I don't like cops."

"You forgot to mention that you worked for Randy Murdoch."

"You never asked."

"Is that where you got the barrel to dispose of Skyler's remains?"

His face crinkled, and his eyes narrowed at me. "What!?"

"We know the barrel was shipped to Randy Murdoch's soap company. You worked there. You had access."

"So?"

"Your girlfriend turns up in one of those barrels, and you don't think that's odd?"

"I think that's fucked up. That's what I think."

"Not looking real good for you right about now, Marshall."

"I don't care how it looks. I didn't kill Skyler. I loved her."

"How about you give us a DNA sample?"

"What's that gonna prove?"

"Paternity. You want to know if it was your kid, don't you? If my girlfriend was murdered, and my child along with her, I'd really want to find the son-of-a-bitch who did it. Unless I was the one who did it." I glared at him.

"I really do want to find out who killed her. It sure as hell wasn't me. And *no*, I ain't giving no DNA."

JD patted Marshall down and pulled out his wallet, keys, a pocket knife, a lighter, and a pack of cigarettes."

"So, what now?" Marshall asked.

"We wait for a patrol car to take you to the station."

"What are you arresting me for?"

"Reckless driving for starters." I read him his rights.

"How about a cigarette while I wait?"

It was like music to my ears. I nodded to JD. He pulled a cigarette from the pack and stuck it in Noonan's mouth. JD used Marshall's lighter to strike it up, and the perp took a deep drag, glowing the cherry-red. The cigarette dangled from his lips while he inhaled on one side of his mouth and exhaled on the other.

That cigarette butt would give us all the DNA we needed to establish paternity. I thought it would be a useful bit of evidence somewhere down the line. It would turn out to be more useful than I had first imagined.

27

After a few minutes, Mendoza arrived. The patrol car pulled in behind us, red and blues flashing.

"Smoke break is over," JD said. "Lose the cigarette."

Marshall spat it to the ground.

I snapped on a pair of nitrile gloves, picked it up, and stuffed it into an evidence collection bag.

Marshall's face twisted. "What the hell are you gonna do with that?"

I smiled. "DNA."

Anger reddened his cheeks. "That's bullshit. You can't do that."

"Yes, I can."

JD stuffed Marshall into the back of the patrol car, and Mendoza took him to the station.

A tow truck arrived to impound the vehicle.

We headed to the station where Marshall was processed, printed, and booked on reckless driving and a host of other charges.

It didn't take him long to start complaining of head, neck, and chest pains. Said his vision was blurred, and he felt nauseous. We called an ambulance, and he was transferred to the emergency room for evaluation. It was probably all BS, but we had to check it out.

We filled out after action-reports, and by that time it was most definitely happy hour.

The band was scheduled to play their last show with Faye later that evening at *Sonic Temple*. We grabbed a quick bite to eat at *Blowfish* and washed it down with a few cocktails before heading over to the practice studio.

The guys were breaking down their gear when we arrived, but Crash hadn't shown up yet. We made short work of it and loaded all the gear into the band van. The rebuilt '70s van was a beast—matte black with chrome pipes, fat Cragar rims, and the *Wild Fury* logo on the side.

I tried calling Crash again, but he didn't answer. I asked Faye, "Have you talked to him?"

She shook her head. "I tried calling a few times. He's giving me the silent treatment."

The guys climbed into the van, and we followed them to *Sonic Temple*. We loaded the gear into the venue. *Wild Fury* had played so many times that the sound guy knew exactly how to set the levels. There was really no need for a sound-check anymore. Just a brief run-through of a song to make sure everything was wired up correctly and functional. We were in and out within an hour, and I still hadn't heard anything from Crash.

The band didn't take the stage until 11 PM, so we had plenty of time to kill. The guys wanted to celebrate their last night with Faye on bass.

The sun had just dipped over the horizon, and the evening was just beginning. We left *Sonic Temple* and walked down Oyster Avenue toward *Overboard*. Tourists started crowding the strip, and the smell of grilled meat and spices filled the air.

The walls at *Overboard* were painted to look like the deep sea with rolling swells. Sharks and other creatures lurked below. The main bar looked like the stern of a ship that was leaving you behind. Blue lights cascaded across the bar in an attempt to make the place feel like you were underwater. The drinks were reasonable, and the music was good.

"Is he just not going to show up?" I said in reference to Crash.

"He doesn't want to be around me," Faye said. "I get it. This is all over after tonight, anyway. I'm out of your hair, and you guys can go back to being what you are."

Dizzy raised his glass to toast. "I know it hasn't exactly been smooth sailing, but we had some good times. Thanks for being part of the journey."

We all clinked glasses and sipped our drinks.

"You're a really solid bass player," Styxx said. It was rare praise coming from him. "I gotta give you that. From a strictly musician standpoint, I've enjoyed it."

"I have no doubt that you're going places with Lip Bomb," JD said.

Faye's eyes misted. "Aw, you guys! You're going to make me cry. I'm gonna miss you."

"It's a small island," JD said. "I'm sure we'll see you around."

Faye gave us all hugs. She wiped her misty eyes and lifted her glass. "Enough of this emotional nonsense. Let's get our drink on!"

We clinked glasses again and stayed at Overboard for a few hours. The band drank more than they should. As usual, Faye seemed to hold her liquor better than most.

It was drawing close to show time, so we stumbled back down the avenue to *Sonic Temple*. The line to get into the venue was around the corner. Sounds of heavy rock filtered out, rumbling the block.

A security guard let us in the back entrance, and we headed to the green room where there was more whiskey, vodka, tequila, and beer. We hung out until *Emissaries of Torment* finished their set. They were a heavy death metal band with painted faces.

The house crew hustled to move their gear off stage to make way for *Wild Fury*.

JD huddled the band, and they all clasped hands. "Let's go out there and blow the roof off this place. Just like it was the

Garden. Let's make Faye's last show with the band memorable."

The band cheered, and we hustled out of the green room as the *Emissaries of Torment* filtered in. They were drenched with sweat, their makeup running. They floated on the high that came from finishing a live performance, smiling and high-fiving each other.

I followed *Wild Fury* to the side of the stage. They gathered for a moment as the lights dimmed. I climbed the steps to the stage and took to the microphone. A single spotlight illuminated me. I had taken on the role of introducing the band in New York, and it stuck. I'd brought on the band ever since, and I didn't see that changing anytime soon.

I hesitated for a moment, looking over the crowd. The blinding light squinted my eyes, and it was difficult to make out discernible features of the audience. But the place was packed.

In my best announcer voice, I said, "Please welcome to the stage, the mighty... Wild Fu-u-u-u-u-ry!"

The crowd erupted.

I rushed off the stage as the band ran on. Styxx took his position behind the candy-apple red drum set.

Dizzy and Faye took their place on either side of the stage.

JD pranced to the microphone.

Lights swirled.

The audience roared.

JD didn't even need to ask, but he did anyway. It had become his signature opener. "Are you ready to rock 'n' roll!?"

Piercing screams filled the venue.

Dizzy clicked off the beat, and the band thundered. Waves of sound crashed over the audience like a tsunami. The crowd was filled with stunning vixens wearing miniskirts, fishnet stockings, and high-heeled shoes. Lots of teased hair and heavy makeup.

As I came off stage, Sadie Savage was waiting for me.

"I'm surprised to see you here," I shouted over the music.

She smiled. "Well, you guys did come out for our show. It's the least I could do."

"Can I get you a drink?"

"I thought you'd never ask," she said.

We weaved our way to the bar. Since most of the patrons were enthralled with the show, there wasn't much delay in getting a drink. I'd worked out a deal with the venue that all our drinks were on the house. They had been providing complimentary beverages in the green room, but not out front. As JD's band gained more clout, it gave us more leverage to negotiate.

The bartender poured two glasses of whiskey and slid them across the counter. I handed one to Sadie, and we clinked glasses.

"To rock 'n' roll," she said.

"To rock 'n' roll."

She looked absolutely delicious. She never lost eye contact with me as she wrapped her lips around the glass and took a sip, leaving a cherry stain. She had a diabolical look in her eyes. "I have a confession to make."

"I'm not a priest, but you can tell me your sins."

She chuckled. "We don't know each other *that* well yet."

I waited eagerly for something juicy.

28

"This isn't my first *Wild Fury* show," Sadie said.

"I snuck out to a few shows before, just to keep tabs on the competition."

"Competition?"

"I wanted to see what you guys were all about."

"Was this before or after Faye joined the band?"

"Faye hasn't joined your band. Just so we're clear. But I saw the band once before and once when she played."

"And what did you think?"

"I thought you guys were good. I'd be lying if I said I wasn't jealous about how quick the band has risen. Faye is good with these guys. She fits in well. It's a great opportunity for her. And it's already drawing more people to our shows. A lot of people come to see Faye, *that chick bass player from Wild Fury*. That's how she's getting known."

"And how do you feel about that?"

"I'm over the whole ego thing. I don't care how or why people find our music. I'm just happy that they do."

We clinked glasses again.

"I'm sure you guys are well on your way," I said.

"That's kinda what I want to talk to you about."

"So, you came just to talk business?"

She frowned at me playfully. "No. I came to show my support. Getting some alone time with the cute manager is a bonus."

I grinned. "You think you can smile at me, bat your eyelashes, and get whatever you want?"

A devilish smirk curled her plump lips. They were slick with gloss and looked tasty. "Yes," she said with a hip shake.

I had a sneaking suspicion that Sadie could get just about whatever she wanted. "So, what kind of business do you want to talk about?"

"You guys did really well with the video for *All I Need*. If we had a video that did a fraction of that, it could really catapult us."

"So you want us to shoot a video for you?"

She gave a hopeful nod.

"I'll consider it," I said, trying not to sound too eager.

"It'll be fun. Hot girls, short skirts, good music. What's not to love?"

"I believe I could be persuaded."

She smiled. "Good. I'll work on persuading you."

We moved away from the bar and hung out at the back of the venue, avoiding the sweaty horde.

Two girls from the *Official Wild Fury Fan Club* sold merchandise from a table at the back of the club. They were happy to do it for free T-shirts and tickets to shows.

Sadie looked at the stacks of T-shirts on the table with envy. "See, that's another thing I need to talk to you about. You guys are really good about the whole *branding* and *merchandising* thing. You sell T-shirts, koozies, key chains, collectors edition vinyl records..."

"Whatever we can think of," I said.

"We leave so much money on the table not doing that kind of thing. Maybe you could give me some pointers."

I smiled. "Maybe I could."

Crash emerged from the crowd and headed toward me.

"You decided to show up," I said, surprised to see him.

He gave me a handshake and a bro hug. "Yeah, sorry, man. I was in a funk for a few days there. I was mad, and I took it out on you. I apologize. I know you were trying to look out for me. Are we cool?"

I smiled. "Yeah. We're cool."

Crash hugged me again.

We hung out and watched the rest of the show. The band rocked out, and the audience went crazy. *Wild Fury* played a couple of encores to thunderous applause, then retired to the green room. We joined them, and there were high-fives all around. There was an awkward moment of tension between Faye and Crash when he first stepped into the room.

"Great show," Crash said, breaking the weirdness. He lifted his arm and displayed his cast. "I'm glad I get this off tomorrow. Too much more of this, and I might be out of a job."

"No way, dude," Dizzy said. "Wild Fury for life!"

"I'm glad you came to see my last performance," Faye said to Crash.

He struggled for words and just nodded.

"You doing okay?"

"Yeah," he said. "I'm hanging in there. It's all good."

"Good." She extended her hand. "Are we friends again?"

"Yeah. Friends."

The two shook, gazing into each other's eyes, that spark still there. Crash held onto her hand for a long time, and she finally slipped it away.

"I'm glad we got that settled," she said, trying to dissipate the awkwardness. "You want a drink?"

"Yeah, sure."

Faye spun around, and her frilly skirt twirled. She grabbed a bottle of whiskey from the table and poured two glasses, then handed one to Crash. She lifted her glass to toast. "It's been a fun ride, gentlemen. And I know I haven't always been easy to deal with."

Sadie chuckled.

Faye's eyes snapped to her. "Shut it," she said playfully. Then continued her speech. "But I'll always look back at this time with fond memories. And I'll be able to say that I played with the mighty Wild Fu-u-u-ry!"

The guys roared and whistled. We all clinked glasses and took a swig.

"Party on the boat!" Dizzy shouted.

I gave a nod, and there was much rejoicing.

We finished our drinks, then loaded out the gear. If *Wild Fury* got much bigger, I was considering hiring a road crew to lug the equipment around. The streaming residuals were trickling in, and they were nothing to sneeze at.

We headed back to the practice studio, unloaded the gear, then drove to the marina. The guys had put the word out before we left *Sonic Temple*, notifying a select group of available women that there would be a late-night soirée. By this point in time, it was well known that the band liked to party after shows, and a growing bevy of groupies would turn up at the marina, invited or not.

The neighbors were always invited to our little gatherings, and we tried to keep the racket to a dull roar. But we did get the occasional complaint. Now and again, someone would call the sheriff, and an envious deputy would show up and tell us to tone it down.

We all stumbled down the dock to the *Avventura*, and I ushered the guests aboard. I took Buddy and Fluffy up to my stateroom to keep them out of the fray, and by the time I returned to the main deck, JD was behind the bar, pouring drinks.

Sadie and I headed up to the sky deck and hung out by the Jacuzzi. There were already a few topless beauties frolicking around in the water, pawing on Dizzy and Styxx. They wasted no time getting things rolling in a positive direction.

Sadie looked impressed. "Living the rock 'n' roll lifestyle, eh?"

I nodded sheepishly. "Somebody's gotta do it."

"You guys sure are having a good time, aren't you?"

I smiled. "We have our ups and downs. Mostly ups."

"How can a girl ever hope to compete with this?" she asked with a seductive glimmer in her eye.

"It's not a competition."

She gave me a sassy look, then bent over gracefully and untied her boots. She had a nice bend. Competition or not, Sadie took it as a challenge. She pulled off her boots and proceeded to peel off her shirt and unclasp her bra. Her glorious orbs sprang free, and my eyes widened.

Her perky peaks jiggled as she shimmied out of her miniskirt. Her pleated plaid garment slid over her luscious hips and fell to the deck, followed by her frilly black panties.

She gave me a naughty glance and shrugged. "When in Rome," she said before strutting toward the Jacuzzi.

She climbed in, and Dizzy and Styxx's eyes rounded.

The jealous groupies they were with quickly refocused their attention by pulling the guys' faces back in the proper direction, planting kisses on their lips.

Sadie looked me dead in the eye. "You coming in?"

There was enough chlorine in the Jacuzzi to kill just about anything. I hoped. It had definitely seen its fair share of action.

It didn't take long for Sadie's wet lips to find mine. Our tongues danced, and my hands explored the inspiring curves of her petite body. It wasn't long before we decided to find a more private location.

Call me modest, but I didn't want to climb out of the Jacuzzi with the captain standing at attention. I gave it a moment for things to settle down, then we climbed out, toweled off, scooped our clothes from the deck, and moved the party to my stateroom. Once inside, we resumed where we left off.

Our bodies collided, and we melted into one another—her warm skin pressed tight against mine, my hands groping delightful mounds of flesh. I led her into the en suite and dialed up a hot shower. We both climbed inside and washed the chlorine off.

Water glistened on her skin, and steam filled the compartment. Her brunette hair was soaked, and mascara streaked down her cheeks as the water poured down. Sadie had a set of lungs, and she sang for me in the shower, putting on a hell of a performance as we made the most of the confined space.

Afterward, we toweled off and slid into my bunk where we cozied up to each other. She curled around me, stroking my skin with her delicate fingers. The rumble of the ongoing party filtered through the bulkheads.

Sadie felt good. There was no doubt about it.

"That was pretty fun," she said. "I might be inclined to do that again sometime."

"Play your cards right, and you just might get lucky."

She smirked. "I think you're the lucky one, Mister."

No argument there.

She leaned in and planted her plump lips on mine. Her delicate fingers traced my abs, gliding south. It didn't take much effort to rekindle the fire. We went for broke again and finally collapsed, fully satiated. I lay there with a heady swirl of whiskey and pleasure chemicals in my brain. Not a bad way to end the night.

I woke in the morning with the shafts of sunlight beaming into the stateroom, painting patterns on the deck. Sadie's naked form curled beside me. It was a nice sight to wake up to.

I slipped out of bed so as not to disturb her, pulled on a pair of shorts, and stumbled down to the main deck. As usual, the place was littered with empty beer bottles and drink glasses. I moved into the galley and put on a pot of coffee, then took Buddy out for a quick walk. I came back and started fixing breakfast.

Crash staggered into the galley. He had a look of pure bliss on his face.

"You seem like you're in a good mood this morning," I said.

"I am."

"What gives?"

"Life has a funny way of working out," he said.

"I take it things went well last night? I saw you and Faye having what seemed to be an intimate conversation."

"Yeah, we kinda worked things out."

"Worked things out like you're friends? Or you're more than friends?"

"We made it official. We're gonna give it a go. We're gonna do the whole *relationship* thing."

I grinned. "I'm happy for you, man."

"Thanks. It was a little rough there for a while, but telling her how I felt was the best thing I could have done."

"Congratulations."

"So, how'd things go with Sadie?"

I just looked at him and smiled, preferring to keep the details to myself.

A grin tugged his lips. "Nice. She's smoking hot." He paused, then his face crinkled. "Doesn't she have a boyfriend?"

I lifted a surprised brow. "She didn't tell me about a boyfriend."

Sadie sauntered into the galley at that point, wearing one of my T-shirts as a dress, her bare feet slapping the deck. "I hear you talking about me. No, I do not have a boyfriend. I got rid of that loser a few weeks ago. Keep up with current events. I'm not a ho." She leaned against the counter and gave us both a sassy look.

Crash raised his hands innocently. "My bad."

"Is this what you boys do after every party, gossip about your conquests?"

We exchanged a sheepish glance, then simultaneously lied, "No."

Sadie rolled her eyes, knowing better. "Don't worry. My girl-friends are gonna ask me about every naughty detail. We're worse than you are."

30

J D stumbled into the galley just in time for breakfast, wiping the sleep from his eyes.

I kept scrambling eggs and frying bacon until everyone was fed.

After breakfast, I said my goodbyes to Sadie and headed over to *Mind, Body & Spirit* with JD. We wanted to drop in on the morning yoga class that Aaron Pennington taught.

The class was full of hot young beauties wearing tight yoga pants and sports bras. They contorted their bodies in all sorts of unnatural yet pleasing positions. The minute we strolled in through the front door, JD muttered under his breath, "Maybe we should offer yoga classes on the boat."

"I think we already do."

He chuckled.

Aaron noticed us with a nervous glance. He moved through the class, adjusting students, making sure they had the appropriate form. He was probably more *hands-on* than he should have been in this day and age, but the ladies didn't seem to mind.

We stood at the back of the class, observing. Relaxing music filtered through the air.

After class, the students rolled up their mats, and a few ladies chatted briefly with Aaron before he made his way over to speak to us. He looked unnerved, as well he should be. He put on a good smile. "Gentlemen, to what do I owe the pleasure?"

"We'd like to talk to you about Vanessa Redman."

His throat tightened. "Who?"

"Cut the crap," JD said. "You know who. You were a person of interest in her husband's murder."

He swallowed hard and glanced around to see if anyone had heard the comment.

The students were filtering out the door, and nobody really paid attention.

"You changed your name and moved to a new town," I said. "Seems suspicious."

"I needed a change of scenery and a fresh start. I didn't have anything to do with Ray Redman's death. You know how rumors start. There was a full investigation. I cooperated with law enforcement. No charges were ever brought."

"That doesn't mean you're innocent."

"What happened to innocent until proven guilty?"

"How long have you been having an affair with Ellie Atwood?" I asked.

"I'm not having an affair with Ellie."

"Really?" I said, incredulous.

"Ellie and I are just friends. I'm trying to offer comfort in her time of need. That's all."

"It would be a lot better for you if you stopped lying."

"I'm not lying."

"You know, Vanessa Redman didn't have anything good to say about you. It's my understanding that you ran off with close to a million dollars of her money."

"I didn't run off with anything. Investments are risky. I fully disclosed the risks to her."

"Ellie is about to come into a sizable sum of money as well. Do you have any investment advice for her?"

The muscles in his jaw flexed. "Like I said, I'm just a friend offering comfort in a trying time."

"Does Ellie know about Vanessa?"

He scoffed. "No, but I'm sure you'll tell her."

"Do you own a gun?"

"No, I do not own a gun."

"It's really hard to keep a secret between multiple people," I said.

"I don't follow."

"You worked with an accomplice for both shootings. You conspired with Vanessa and maybe Ellie. How long before one of them flips?"

"No one is going to flip because there was no conspiracy. Your theory is ridiculous."

"I've known Ellie for a long time. I'll admit, the whole affair blindsided me. I didn't see it coming. Apparently, Chuck didn't either."

"There was nothing to see coming," he protested.

"Ellie is going to crack under the pressure. And the pressure will increase. The only reason Vanessa didn't rat you out was because she didn't want to get charged with conspiracy to commit murder."

Aaron's cheeks reddened. "I've got nothing further to say to you."

I smiled. "We'll see you around."

JD and I left the yoga studio and stepped onto the sidewalk. The fresh morning air blew down the avenue.

"That bastard is guilty as sin," JD said. "It's written all over his face."

I looked through the large glass windows of the Yoga studio. Aaron's nervous eyes flicked about as he made a phone call.

"I bet he's calling Ellie right now, doing damage control."

"I think we should check in on her," JD said.

31

"Oh, hi guys," Ellie said when she pulled open the door. "I wish you would have let me know you were stopping by. I'm just about to head out."

She frowned.

"This will only take a minute," I said.

She noted my tone. "Is this a social visit or case related?"

"A little of both," I said.

"Have you found something?"

"We're closing in," I said.

"Fantastic. What can you tell me?"

I exchanged a glance with JD.

"You mind if we come inside?"

"Sure." She stepped aside and let us into the foyer. She closed the door and looked at her watch.

"I hope we won't make you late," I said.

She shook her head. "No. Nothing is more important than this."

"About Aaron," I said.

"I know things must have looked awkward the other night. Aaron is a dear friend. He's really been supportive and has been someone I could talk to lately."

"Aaron might not be who you think he is," I said.

Her face crinkled. "What do you mean?"

"Well, for starters, his last name isn't Pennington. It's Patterson." I told her the story of Vanessa Redman.

Her jaw dropped.

"Still want to tell me there's nothing going on between you two?" I asked. "Now is the time to come clean. Otherwise, you're just digging yourself deeper."

She hesitated for a moment. Then exhaled a guilty breath. "Okay. Yes. I've been having an affair with Aaron for about six months now." She cringed. "I know you must think I'm a horrible person. The truth is that Chuck and I were having problems. He wanted one thing, and I wanted another."

"Clearly," JD muttered.

She shot him a look. "I don't know how to explain it. It just happened."

"You just slipped and fell into Aaron's lap," JD said dryly.

"I know you guys were close to Chuck. You must think I'm a monster. But I swear to you, I did not conspire to kill my husband. You really think Aaron had something to do with Ray Redman's death?"

We both nodded.

"And you think he was involved in Chuck's death?"

We both nodded again.

She sighed. "I don't know what to think."

"Has he talked to you about potential investments?"

"He mentioned that he thought I could make a lot of money in cryptocurrency. He said if I wanted, he could show me how to 10x my money."

JD and I shared a glance.

"I don't really understand the stuff." She paused. "You're saying he ran off with a million dollars of that woman's money, right?"

"It appears that way."

I wasn't sure if she was playing dumb or if she had been duped.

Her eyes welled, and tears spilled over. "So, Aaron never really cared about me?"

"Doubtful."

"I'm such a fool."

If she was acting, she put on a good show.

"I hope for your sake you're not involved."

She shook her head, sobbing. "I wasn't. I would never do something like that to Chuck."

JD stifled an eye roll.

"We're gonna find out who killed your husband," I said. "Bank on it."

She swallowed hard. "I hope you do. Then you'll know I didn't have anything to do with it."

There was a long, awkward silence.

"Well, I don't want to keep you from your appointment," I said.

We let ourselves out and strolled the walkway to the Porsche.

"Think she's lying?" JD asked.

"Time will tell."

We climbed into the car, and JD pulled from the curb. I decided it was time to track down Tommy Halford. He lived on a yacht in the marina at the country club. The slip fees were exorbitant. From what I could tell, he'd done well for himself in the tech industry.

We headed across the island, pulled into the posh club, cruising past well-manicured fairways and trimmed greens. Members zipped around in electric golf carts.

We drove to the parking lot by the main clubhouse. The lot was filled with exotic cars, expensive SUVs, and luxury sedans.

We hopped out and ambled down the path to the marina. It was filled with superyachts, sleek racing boats, and 50-foot sailboats that could take you around the globe.

We wandered around, looking for the *Make'n Bacon*.

A female voice called out to JD. I recognized the voice instantly, and it made me cringe.

32

The sultry voice belonged to JD's ex-girlfriend, Sloan—the girl that he fell head over heels for. The one he proposed to after only a few weeks, intending to make her number seven in his list of ex-wives. Sadly, or fortunately, depending upon how you look at it, she turned him down. I'd never seen JD take it so hard. He was in a funk for weeks.

She caught up to us, wearing a short golf skirt, tight top, and visor. The stunning brunette was the *total package*. It was easy to see why JD had fallen so hard. But she never quite warmed up to the idea of commitment for various reasons. Her career as a pro golfer took precedent.

"I thought that was you," she said. "I haven't seen you in forever."

"It's been a minute," JD said.

"How are you doing?"

JD smiled. "I'm good."

"I see your video bouncing around social media. I heard the show in New York went well. You guys are on your way."

"It seems like it."

"What are you gonna do when you reach the top?"

JD shrugged. "Enjoy it while it lasts."

"Good answer."

"What about you? How have you been?"

"Things are good. The tour is going well. Moving up in the rankings."

The diamond ring on her finger sparkled, and Jack almost had a conniption fit. His face flushed, and his jaw tensed. He tried to hide it, but his eyes welled. When he spoke, his throat was tight.

"That's a nice ring," JD said, his eyes shooting laser beams.

Sloan grew self-conscious and suddenly didn't know what to do with her hands. She fluttered them about. "Oh, yeah. It just kinda happened."

"I see. Who's the lucky guy?"

"Nobody you know."

The veins in Jack's neck pulsed. I could see his blood pressure rising.

"His name is Christian Hutton. He lives here in the marina. I was just on my way to see him," she said, pointing down the dock at a superyacht.

There was a long, awkward silence.

"Well, it was good to see you both," she said. "I'm glad you're doing well. Take care."

She continued down the dock, her white golf skirt bouncing in delightful ways.

JD and I watched her go.

I patted him on the back. "Let it go, brother. Let it go."

He shook his head. "She wasn't ready for commitment when I asked her."

"She wasn't ready for a commitment... *with you*," I added.

He scowled at me.

I raised my hands innocently. "I'm just saying. You got off easy."

JD grumbled some more as we strolled down the dock to the *Make'n Bacon*. It was a 140-foot *Benedetti* with a Navy blue hull and windswept lines. It was sleek and modern with large windows and scantily clad beauties lounging on the forward sun pads.

We crossed the passerelle to the aft deck. There was an alfresco dining area with ample seating. We banged on the glass door to the salon and waited. A few moments later, a guy in his early 50s with dark hair slid open the door, a piña colada dangling from his hand.

He wore tropical-print board shorts and no shirt. Despite being in his 50s, he looked jacked—well-defined muscles and not an ounce of fat. He had a square jaw, brown eyes, and didn't look anything like the nerdy kid he did in high school. He was definitely on the *juice*.

I flashed my badge, and we made our introductions.

Tommy looked us up and down for a minute and said, "You're here about Skyler, aren't you?"

I nodded.

He stepped out of the salon and offered us a seat at the settee. "Can I get you anything to drink?"

"No, thank you," I replied, taking a seat.

"I heard you found her in a barrel? You got anything to go on?"

"We have a few leads," I said.

"How can I help?"

"We talked to Tiffany McKnight."

His eyes rounded. "Man, she was something."

"From what I understand, you had a thing for Skyler."

He laughed. "I did. I was so in love with that girl. I didn't even know what love was then. Hell, I don't even know what love is now, but I keep looking for it."

He flashed a sly smile.

"Looks like you've done pretty well for yourself."

"No complaints here."

"I heard you were so infatuated with Skyler that you'd spy on her."

He laughed again. "Statute's up, right?"

I nodded.

"Yeah, I guess I did some crazy shit when I was younger. But you know, hormones."

"Did those hormones make you kill her and stuff her into a barrel?"

He smiled. "Come on, really? I can't be your lead. Surely you've got better suspects than me. How about Marshall Noonan? Total loser. That guy always had my vote for a closet serial killer. And just look at how he turned out. I could have sworn I saw him begging for change on a street corner a few months ago."

"Where were you the night Skyler disappeared?"

"Wow, really? You guys are serious?"

"Doing our due diligence."

He thought about it and nodded. "Okay. I can respect that. It was a long time ago, but I'll never forget where I was. If I recall correctly, that was a Thursday night, and I was playing Dungeons & Dragons with Conrad Simmons and Gene Dixon, and I think John Foster was there, but I'm not sure."

"Did you two ever date? Hookup?"

"I wish. Skyler was way out of my league. Of course, nothing's out of my league now."

"Do you know if she was involved with anyone else besides Marshall?"

"Marshall was her boyfriend."

"That's not what I asked."

"I know what you asked." He paused. "Yeah, she saw somebody else."

"Older guy. Married, right?"

"I don't know if he was married or not, but he was an older guy." He paused and took a breath. "This was a couple weeks before she disappeared. I never told the cops about it at the time. I didn't want to sound like some kind of stalker. They interviewed a lot of kids at school. I feel bad about not saying anything. But I followed her one night."

He hung his head, embarrassed.

"Care to elaborate?"

33

"**I** don't know why, but I used to drive by her house all the time just to see if she was home," Tommy said.

"And peep on her sometimes," I added.

"Can you blame me? That girl was hot, and she had great perky little..." He censored himself before continuing. "Anyway, one night, I saw her sneak out of her window and get into a car with this guy."

"What kind of car?"

"I'll never forget. It was such a cool car at the time—a candy-apple red convertible Cadillac. An Eldorado Biarritz. Sweet pimpmobile. Anyway, they drove around for a while, and he took her down to Taffy Beach. They walked along the shore, he took her under the pier, and they did the old *in and out*. At first, I was really pissed off. But then I found myself turned on by the whole thing. Weird, but whatever. They went at it for a while, then finished up. He drove her home. That was it."

"Did you see them together any other time?"

"No. That was the only time."

"Did you recognize the guy?"

"No. I'd never seen him before."

"You think you'd recognize him if I showed you a picture from the era?"

Tommy shrugged. "I don't know. Maybe. It's not like I had binoculars. I didn't get that close."

"You're sure about the make and model of the car?"

"Positive. I thought it was so cool at the time. I wanted one bad." He grinned. "But I have much nicer things now."

A topless blonde made her way down the port side passage to the aft deck. She wore big sunglasses, small bikini bottoms, and nothing else. She looked like she'd stepped off the pages of a magazine. Tight, toned abs, long legs that shimmered with lotion, bubbly assets. She was probably 23. She made a pouty face and spoke in a breathy, baby doll voice—the kind of voice you'd do just about anything for. "We're out of strawberry daiquiris. Can you make us some more?"

She turned out her bottom lip.

Tommy looked at us and shrugged. "Duty calls, gentlemen."

He pushed away from the table and stood up. He escorted us to the passerelle, then attended to his plaything.

We crossed to the dock, and I dialed Denise. "I need you to look up old DMV records."

I gave her the make and model of the car and asked her to look up Randy Murdoch's registration history.

"I'll let you know what I find out," she said.

JD glared at the superyacht that belonged to Christian Hutton as we walked back to the parking lot.

"Let it go," I said.

JD frowned at me. "What!? It's gone. I'm over it."

He clearly wasn't.

We hopped into the car and drove to the station. We found Denise at her desk.

"Guess what?"

"Randy Murdoch owned a convertible Cadillac in 1989," I said, hopeful.

She smiled. "Yup, and get this. That car was an '84, and was a limited edition run. There were only a few thousand convertibles like it ever made, and Randy's car was the only one registered in Coconut Key at the time. It's a safe bet that Randy Murdoch is *the married man*."

A confident smirk tugged my lips. "That ought to be enough for a warrant."

We filled out sworn affidavits, went to the judge, and asked for a warrant. It seemed like a slam dunk. The judge agreed, but it took some convincing.

I didn't think we'd need a tactical team to bring in Randy Murdoch, but Faulkner and Erickson accompanied us. Bringing him back to the station in the back of the Porsche wasn't really an option.

Mrs. Murdoch was understandably concerned to see the four of us standing on her front porch, asking about her husband again.

I displayed the warrant, and her eyes rounded, and her jaw dropped. The color drained from her face, and she fumbled for words. "That's not possible," she stammered. "Randy can't be involved in that girl's disappearance."

"Death, ma'am. Death," I said. "Is he here?"

She shook her head, still dazed. I nodded to Erickson and Faulkner. They marched inside and quickly searched the home.

I told her that we had a witness that had seen Randy with the girl. I didn't go into much detail.

"Your witness is lying. I refuse to believe such a thing."

Erickson and Faulkner returned a moment later. Faulkner shook his head. "He's not here, but I did find this."

He held a picture frame in his hand. The faded photo was of a 1980s era Randy standing in front of a red convertible Cadillac, wearing a mustache and a grey Members Only jacket. The photo looked like it could have been an ad for the car, the jacket, or cigarettes.

Mrs. Murdoch's eyes narrowed. "You can't take that! That's personal."

"We'll return it," I promised. "Where's your husband, Mrs. Murdoch?"

"Do I have to tell you?"

"You don't want to be charged with obstruction of justice, do you?"

Her face tightened. "He's at the country club," she sighed. "Playing golf."

"Thank you."

"You're wrong, Deputy. You're wrong about this, and I hope you know that you're about to destroy a man. A hard-working family man."

Her words stung. Her life was about to be upended through no fault of her own. I didn't like this part of the job. But I didn't like seeing innocent people murdered either.

We plunged down the steps, raced across the courtyard, and pushed through the wrought-iron gate.

I took a picture of the photo so I'd have it handy on my phone, then gave it back to Faulkner to log.

We hopped into the Porsche, and Faulkner and Erickson followed us to the country club in their patrol car. We stopped in the pro shop.

The golf pro confirmed Randy's tee time. He gave us an estimate of where he thought Randy might currently be on the course. He gave us a map and the keys to a couple golf carts. We hopped in and raced down the concrete path, backtracking from the 18th hole.

The electric carts whined as we weaved down the path alongside green fairways, winding our way to the 15th green.

Two carts were parked by a sand trap, and a foursome played out the hole. One of Randy's buddies tended the pin while he sunk a 12-foot putt with a smooth stroke.

The little white ball fell into the hole and rattled with a satisfying clunk.

Randy had a wide smile on his face and pulled a triumphant fist. His grin soon faded as we approached the green. His eyes rounded. It was clear by our demeanor we were here to bring him in.

"Randy Murdock, you're under arrest for the murder of Skyler Locke," I said.

His jaw dropped, and he blinked rapidly. "That's incorrect. You've got the wrong guy."

Faulkner slapped the cuffs around his wrists and ratcheted them tight while his friends looked on in dismay.

"Don't say a word," one of them cautioned. "I'll call Carl."

I assumed Carl was an attorney friend of theirs.

Faulkner escorted Murdoch to the golf cart and sat him in the passenger seat. Erickson climbed onto the back of the vehicle where the golf clubs would normally reside. He held on tight as Faulkner drove down the path toward the clubhouse.

"You're making a big mistake," Murdoch's friend said.

I shrugged and walked down the slope of the green to our golf cart. JD hopped behind the wheel, put it into gear, and mashed the pedal, spitting a few blades of grass.

Club members gawked with wide eyes as Faulkner stuffed Randy into the back of the patrol car near the clubhouse. This kind of thing was a rare sight at the posh country club.

At the station, Murdoch was processed, printed, and put into an interrogation room. At this point, I didn't expect him to talk, but it was worth a try.

34

Randy Murdoch looked a little peaked under the pale green glow of the fluorescent lights. Sweat misted on his skin, and his nervous eyes surveyed us with trepidation as we entered the room.

The chair squeaked across the tile as I pulled it away from the table and sat down across from him.

"I'm not saying a word without an attorney present."

He didn't specifically *ask* to speak with an attorney. "Okay. That's fine. But just FYI, we know you were having an affair with Skyler Locke."

He balked. "That's preposterous. I barely knew the girl."

"I thought you said you didn't know her."

He swallowed hard.

"We've got an eyewitness that saw you pick her up in your red Cadillac. You took her to the beach. You did something you shouldn't have under the pier."

His face went long, and his eyes widened. He was silent for a long moment. "An eyewitness from 30 some-odd years ago? No way that holds up. And the statute of limitations has long since expired."

"First-degree felony where the victim was under 18. No limitations."

Randy swallowed hard.

"She was pregnant with your child."

His throat tightened again. "You can't prove that."

"Actually, we can. I'll get a court order for your DNA. It's not looking good, Randy."

The sweat on his brow intensified.

"You know what I think? I think Skyler told you she was pregnant, and you freaked out."

He said nothing.

"I think you were worried that your entire life would come crumbling down. You'd go to jail, your wife would leave you, your business would collapse. So you killed Skyler, stuffed her in a barrel that you had around the warehouse, took her out on your boat, and got rid of her."

He shook his head. "I did no such thing."

"Why don't you do us all a favor and come clean? Cooperate, and maybe we can get you some kind of deal. You can live out the rest of your days in a minimum-security prison. Hell, it might almost be like a country club."

I pulled out a DNA testing kit that contained a swab sealed in a container. I put on a pair of nitrile gloves, tore open the package, removed the sterile Q-tip, and said, "I need to swab the inside of your cheek. It will only take a second, and it won't hurt."

"No."

I will go to the judge, and I will come back with a warrant for this. We will prove that you're the father."

He glared at me, silent a long moment.

"Fine. Take your sample. But I didn't kill Skyler, and you can't prove that I did. When this is all said and done, I'm going to walk out of here, and you won't be able to touch me."

I grinned. "Wanna bet?"

35

We dropped the DNA sample at the lab, filled out after-action reports, then headed to *Diver Down* to get something to eat. We took a seat at the bar, and Teagan had two beers waiting. "What's with the glum faces?"

I shrugged. "We just arrested an 80-year-old guy for murder."

"The barrel girl?"

I nodded. "The guy got away with it for 30-plus years. If all goes as planned, he'll spend his last days in a 6x8 cell."

"That should be a reason to celebrate. Late justice is better than no justice," she said. "Plus, when you wrap this up, it'll give the family closure."

"Closure ain't gonna bring the girl back," I said with a frown.

A breaking news alert flashed on the TV behind the bar. Paris Delaney's gorgeous face appeared on the screen. "A retired businessman has been arrested in connection with the death of Skyler Locke. As we reported earlier, the young girl's body was found at sea, contained in a steel drum. Randy Murdoch was arrested at the Coconut Key Country Club earlier today."

Randy's mugshot flashed on the screen. It was readily available from the county website under the recent arrests tab. The image of Randy wearing his Members Only jacket in front of the red convertible flashed on the screen next. Somebody in the department had taken a picture of it and texted Paris a copy.

"The investigation is ongoing, and we will continue to give you updates as the story develops. For Action News, I'm Paris Delaney."

"Do you guys know what you want to eat?" Teagan asked.

We perused the menu and placed our order. We started with chips and the crab, spinach, and artichoke dip. JD ordered the stone crab claws, and I got a crab cake sandwich.

Denise called during lunch. "You're not gonna like this. You know that kid you arrested for DUI the other night?"

"Yeah, Cameron Hartsell. What about him?"

"The charges were dropped."

I lifted an astonished brow. "All of them?"

"All of them. Got a slap on the wrist. His lawyer worked out some kind of non-prosecution agreement. Got off with a fine."

"Saved again by daddy's money."

"That's not all," she said. "I started digging. There are a lot of cases getting dismissed or receiving lesser penalties."

"What's that about?"

"It seems Coconut County's State Attorney is letting these people off easy if they make contributions to the Forward Fund."

"Is that legal?"

"Not on the federal level. Settlements to third parties are prohibited under the Federal rules of criminal procedure. But for state crimes, it seems they get a pass."

"That sounds ripe for a conflict of interest," I said. "Keep digging into that. See what you can find."

"Well, you'll have a chance to talk with Stella at tonight's charity event."

"Oh, right," I said.

"I thought you might have forgotten about that."

"No, I didn't forget. It just left my mind."

She chuckled. "I'll talk to you later."

I relayed the information to JD.

His face twisted with an annoyed scowl. "I swear, there's more corruption in this town..."

I called Isabella, my contact at Cobra Company. I asked her to drum up as much information as she could about Stella Turner and the Coconut Key Forward Fund.

"Investigating charities now?" she asked.

"See where it leads." I filled her in on the situation. "Any word on Elias Fink or Sophia Breslin?"

"No, but I've got my ears to the ground. Trust me. I'll let you know as soon as they pop up on my radar."

We finished lunch, then headed back to the *Avventura* and cleaned up the mess from the after-party. I usually got stuck holding the bag in that department, so I was pleased to have a little help from JD.

We had a free afternoon, so we took the boat out, fished, searched for the lost treasure of Jacques De La Fontaine, and drank a few beers. We headed back to Coconut Key in time to get dressed for the evening.

JD headed home to make himself look more presentable. It was a black-tie fundraiser, and I dusted off my Di Fiore tux, put on my cummerbund and tie, and styled my hair.

Denise swung by the marina in her banana yellow SUV to pick me up. She texted me when she pulled into the lot, and I strolled down the dock and climbed into the passenger seat. She looked divine in a black strapless evening gown that hugged her petite form. Pearls dangled from her elegant neck, and her emerald eyes sparkled.

"I might not be totally embarrassed to be seen with you," I teased.

She sneered at me. Her eyes surveyed my attire. "Yeah, well, you're not a total embarrassment either. I could do worse."

I laughed.

We drove out of the lot and headed over to JD's. Denise pulled into the circular drive and honked the horn.

JD emerged a few moments later wearing a tuxedo with a Hawaiian-print cummerbund and tie. His hair was slicked back into a tight ponytail, and he wore dark sunglasses. He looked like a cross between a sleazy record producer and a covert agent. Neither was far from the truth.

He climbed into the backseat, and we zipped across the island to the *Seven Seas*.

Jack inhaled a deep breath. "I see you got the smell out of the car."

"I took it to your friend. They detailed it inside and out. Did a paint correction, buffed out all the scratches, and put a ceramic coating on it."

"It looks nice," JD said. "I wish my car looked this nice."

"What are you gonna do about that?"

"I haven't had time to take it in yet."

We pulled into the lot at the luxury hotel. Attendees in formal evening attire hopped out of luxury vehicles at the valet stand, and parking attendants hustled cars through the lot. There was a long line of cars, and the valets had used orange parking cones to take up every available space in the lot, forcing you to use the valet at $28.50 a pop.

Jackasses.

It took 15 minutes to get through the line. An attendant grabbed Denise's door and handed her a ticket, while another grabbed mine and JD's.

We hopped out, straightened our jackets, and strolled into the lobby. We moved past the waterfall, past the elevator banks, and headed toward the pool.

Coconut County's elite mixed and mingled. A quartet played classical music, and a small stage was set up with a podium and PA speakers. Palm trees swayed overhead, and the pool was illuminated.

I saw Daniels across the pool, mingling. He hated these kinds of things, but elections weren't cheap, and it was always good to keep up relationships.

We made a beeline for the bar and took advantage of the complimentary drinks. There was a silent auction, and people bid on various collectibles and jewelry that had been donated.

We perused the items and waited for the event to begin. It was a little after 7:30 PM when Stella Turner took the stage. "Good evening, ladies and gentlemen. Thank you all for coming. I am so excited to share with you all of the great accomplishments we've made this past year. The fund has given out over $3 million in grants and is reshaping the community for the better."

The crowd cheered.

Stella smiled. "With your help, we can continue to do great things, so I know you will dig deep and give all that you can. Think of it as an investment in the future of Coconut Key. Thank you all, and enjoy the evening."

The crowd roared with applause.

Stella left the stage with a bright smile, mixing and mingling, glad-handing the mega-donors.

I approached and hovered in the wings, waiting for the opportune time to strike.

"I think it's truly amazing what you've been able to accomplish," I said, putting on my best phony smile. I figured I'd go in soft. Drop the hammer later.

"Why, thank you, Deputy..."

"Wild."

"Yes, Wild." Stella smiled. "I'm just passionate about this community."

"It shows, but let me ask you something. Cameron Hartsell... We recently arrested him for DUI, reckless driving, and a host of other charges. I believe you negotiated a non-prosecution agreement in exchange for a sizable contribution to the fund."

Stella forced a smile. "Yes. As I recall, it was his first offense."

"No. It wasn't his first offense."

"Regardless, given the circumstances, I thought the nature of the fine would be a significant deterrent to future violations.

The boy is also a college student, and in the interest of his academic study, I thought this was the best arrangement for all parties involved."

"It's not really a *fine*, is it? More of a *contribution*."

"We can argue the semantics of it all day long, but at the end of the day, this fund is benefiting the community. We are providing assistance to the homeless, meals for the elderly, educational supplies for underprivileged children, the list goes on. Deputy Wild, I've been doing this job long enough to know that once somebody gets into the system, they have a very hard time getting out. It's my belief that we should do everything possible to keep offenders out of the system and use our resources to rehabilitate them and deter future criminal behavior."

"And I can appreciate that. But what happens next time Cameron goes out drinking with his buddies and kills someone."

Her face tensed. "Let's pray a tragedy like that never happens."

She moved on, smiled, and shook someone else's hand. That was the end of our conversation.

JD muttered in my ear, "I'm beginning not to like her."

"I'm gonna keep digging," Denise said. "There's something shady about the whole thing."

"You're telling me," JD said.

We hung out until the free drinks ended, then the three of us decided to hit Oyster Avenue. Since we were dressed up, we ended up at *Keys*—an upscale piano bar. There were lots of diamond necklaces, slinky evening gowns, and spike-heeled shoes. We fit right in.

We grabbed a drink from the bar.

The murmur of chatter mixed with smooth jazz.

My phone buzzed with a call from Sheriff Daniels. "We found the silver sedan."

"Where?"

"Mendoza spotted it at the Mega Mart. He happened to be cruising through, and it caught his eye. The shooters must have dumped it there and gotten into another vehicle. It had April McGee's plates on it. Forensics is dusting the car for prints now, and Mendoza is trying to get security footage of the lot. They found 9mm shell casings in the passenger seat. It's looking like this is definitely the car that did the drive-by on Chuck. Hopefully, we can pull a print from the shell casings."

"That's great news."

"I didn't have time to speak with you at the charity event. I saw you talking to Stella Turner. What was that about?"

"Just a friendly conversation."

"I don't think she thought it was too friendly. She told me she didn't like being harassed by my deputies about the way she prosecutes cases."

"I didn't harass her. I just asked questions."

"Try not to ruffle too many feathers. We're on the same team."

"Have you looked into her Forward Fund?"

"No. I attend her fundraisers, and I write a check every year. That's it."

"Maybe you should do a little more research. I know I am."

"If you think she's doing something inappropriate, get proof. Otherwise, keep your damn mouth shut."

I bit my tongue. "You got it, boss."

He hated it when I called him that.

I ended the call and slipped the phone back into my pocket. I griped to my compatriots, "Daniels says don't rock the boat."

JD scoffed. "That's what we do best."

"We'll just keep this investigation between us," Denise said with a smile.

She lifted her glass, and we clinked.

A table opened up nearby, and we grabbed it. A busboy came by a moment later, cleared the empty drinks, and wiped the table down. We lounged around, listening to the piano player tickle the ivories, accompanied by a jazz trumpet player.

An idea popped into my head. Maybe it was the jazz. Maybe the whiskey. But the neurons were firing. I sent a text to Paris Delaney. This kind of thing was right up her alley. She could stir up trouble, and it wouldn't blow back on us. [What do you know about the Forward Fund?]

[*O**h, so you want to talk to me now?*] Paris texted back.

[I talk to you all the time.]

She responded with an eye-roll emoji.

[Just thought it might be something you'd be interested in.]

[No comment. That's all you ever say now.]

[Not true. I gave you plenty of details about Deputy Atwood.]

[Whatever.]

[Do you want a scoop, or not?]

I waited for her to respond.

[I don't know if I'd call it a scoop when you're asking me for information. Do you have anything juicy?]

I excused myself from the table, stepped outside where it was quieter, and dialed her number. I didn't want to put my thoughts in writing, especially when speaking about a state attorney. No telling where a screengrab might turn up or who else might see it.

"Oh, a phone call," Paris said with surprise. "I'm honored."

"Are you recording this call?"

"No."

"You should look into the non-prosecution and deferred-prosecution agreements being made," I said. "See where the funds are going and how they are being used."

"Are you alleging corruption?"

"I'm not alleging anything. I'm just suggesting that you do what you do best."

"Careful, Deputy Wild. That almost sounds like a compliment."

"I acknowledge talent when I see it."

"You know I have other talents," she said in a seductive voice.

"I'm aware."

"Maybe we should grab a drink and discuss this further."

"Can't right now."

"What could possibly be more enticing than a deep, intellectual conversation about public corruption?" she teased.

"I'm out with friends."

"Ditch them."

"Tempting."

"Don't you want to work out all those pent-up frustrations? You can go back to hating me in the morning."

I chuckled.

"Shit, hang on." She clicked to the other line, then clicked back a moment later. "Sorry. Gotta run. Major car crash."

"Never let a tragedy go to waste," I snarked.

"We'll resume this discussion later," she said before hanging up.

I stepped back inside and returned to our table. I was met with curious eyes.

"What was that about?" JD asked.

"I put a little bug in Paris's ear about Stella Turner."

JD smirked. "Not a bad idea. That girl loves to look for trouble."

"Be careful, Tyson. You make a deal with the devil, you might get burned."

We had another drink, then called it an early night. Denise had an early shift. She drove us back to the marina and dropped me off first.

I said my goodbyes, and Denise took JD home.

The boats swayed in their slips as I strolled down the dock. I got a call from Sadie along the way. "Hey, what are you doing?"

"Just getting home."

"I may need you to return the favor."

"What favor?"

"I might need to borrow your bass player."

My brow knitted. "Why? What happened?"

"Faye is no longer in the band."

"What!?"

"We kicked her out."

"Why?"

"Because she hooked up with Katie's boyfriend."

My jaw dropped, and my eyes widened. "Seriously?"

"Seriously."

"When did this happen?"

"Apparently when she and Crash were split."

"Does Crash know about this yet?"

"I don't know. I haven't told him. I'll leave that up to your discretion."

I cringed. I did not want to get in the middle of this drama. I took a deep breath, and my head fell into my hands as I thought about the scenario. "Are you sure they hooked up?"

"Hey, I wasn't there. I didn't see it. I guess Katie and her boyfriend got into a fight, and the truth came out. He admitted it to her. Then Katie confronted Faye. This all went down before we were supposed to go on stage. The two of them went at each other in the green room, and we had to pull them apart."

"What did you guys do about the show?"

"Lexi and I went on stage and played an acoustic set. Katie refused to play with Faye, and they both stormed off."

"That sucks."

"You're telling me."

"What are you going to do?"

"Try to find a replacement ASAP. But as you know, that's no easy task." She sighed. "You guys got lucky things didn't implode with Faye."

"They, kind of, did. And I'm not sure we're clear of the fallout yet," I said.

I crossed the passerelle to the aft deck and pulled open the sliding door. Buddy bounced and barked, and I knelt down and petted him while I talked on the phone.

"I'm not trying to make this a regular thing, but are you up for a late-night visit?"

"I believe I can accommodate that request."

"Good, I need to work out some stress."

I chuckled. "You know where to find me."

I ended the call and headed up to my stateroom. I peeled out of the tux and put on a pair of shorts and a T-shirt. I grabbed Buddy's leash and took him out for a quick walk.

Sadie showed up as I was heading back toward the boat. She hopped out of her SUV and sauntered toward me, looking like the alternative rock goddess that she was—white cut-up T-shirt, black lacy bra, black miniskirt, fishnet stockings, Dr. Martens.

"Oh, my gawd!" she groaned. "What a night."

She flung her arms around me and planted a juicy kiss on my lips. "Make it all better, Daddy."

I was certainly going to try.

38

I woke up in the morning with the punk rock vixen naked beside me. Not a bad way to wake up. We spent the morning rolling around the sheets, working out every last bit of stress. We took a shower and worked out a little more amid the steamy water.

Afterward, we toweled off, got dressed, and made our way down to the galley, where I fixed breakfast. We sat at the settee, chowing down on ham and cheese omelettes.

"I saw the bass in your room. Crash says you're actually pretty good."

"I'm just noodling around for fun."

"You might be able to solve our bass player problem."

I gave her a suspicious glance. "How so?"

"Want to be the only dude in an all-girl band?"

I laughed. "I'm not on that level."

"You might surprise yourself."

"Crash is a much better player than I am. Ask him."

"I don't know if he's gonna want to sit in with our band after everything that's happened."

I shrugged.

"The songs are pretty simple. I bet you could pick them up quickly. It would just be temporary until we found a permanent replacement."

"You can't really be serious?"

"I'm dead serious. Do you know how hard it is to find a talented, reliable bass player that's not a drug addict?"

"Trust me, I know."

"Plus, you're kinda hot." She smiled. "You'll draw in more female fans and expand our base. I only have one rule. Not that I'm trying to place restrictions on you or anything, but I'm the only babe in the band you can bang. Deal?"

"I'll think about it."

"You'll think about whether you can refrain from screwing my bandmates? Or, you'll think about the gig?"

"Your bandmates *are* pretty hot."

She smirked. "They are. How will you ever manage?" she snarked.

"So far, the lead singer is keeping me occupied."

"Don't think about it too long. We've got a show next week, and we need to practice."

"You haven't heard me play."

"If Crash says you're pretty good, you're pretty good. Plus, I have a feeling about you. There's untapped potential there," she said with a naughty grin.

"There are too many things to go wrong with this scenario," I said.

"What's to go wrong? I can keep my personal feelings in check if you can. Business is business. Pleasure is pleasure."

"It seems like your drummer couldn't separate business from personal."

"You're not screwing my drummer. You're screwing me. And after the temper tantrum she threw last night, I might be looking for a new drummer too. Don't get me wrong, I like Katie, she's fantastic. What Faye did was inexcusable. I just wish Katie would have confronted her after the show instead of before."

"Matters of the heart are often hard to control."

"I understand. I'm just saying..."

"Call Crash. Ask him to sit in."

"I'm not gonna be the one to call him up and explain the reason why we fired Faye."

I groaned. "I really don't want to be the bearer of bad news in this situation."

"Somebody needs to tell him."

"It's gonna devastate him."

Sadie frowned.

"I'll call him after a while," I said. "I need time to plan this out."

"He might already know. Maybe Faye came clean with him."

My phone buzzed with a call from Denise. I swiped the screen and put the phone to my ear.

"I got some interesting news," she said. "Before I get to the good stuff... Cameron Hartsell was arrested last night for DUI. He totaled another car."

"That must have been the story Paris was chasing. Maybe this one will stick."

"Let's hope so."

"Ok, give me the good stuff."

"Marshall Noonan's DNA did not match the fetus in the Skyler Locke case. However, we got a hit on an unsolved rape case up in Pineapple Bay. It was a positive match for Noonan. Looks like he's going back to the can for a long time."

A satisfied smirk curled my lips. "Well, what do you know?"

"There's more... We don't have Randy Murdoch's DNA analysis back yet, but I can tell you he's not going to match."

My brow crinkled. "Why do you say that?"

"According to Brenda, there are matching strands that could only come from a family relation."

That hung there for a second.

My stomach twisted. "You mean..." I didn't even want to say it out loud.

"Yup. There's only one person that could be the father of that baby. Daniels is working on getting a warrant now. He wants you and JD to get down to the station. Take Erickson and Faulkner, and bring that guy in."

"With pleasure."

39

There was no need to break down Paul Locke's door. No need to storm his house with tactical gear and assault rifles. With his bad hip, Paul was in no condition to put up a fight.

I knocked on the door, and he answered a few minutes later. Concern twisted his face when he saw Erickson and Faulkner standing behind us. Uniformed deputies often have that effect.

"What can I do for you, gentlemen?" he asked with an air of trepidation.

"You're under arrest for sexual battery," I said.

His face crinkled. "What!?"

"Turn around and put your hands behind your head."

"You've made some kind of mistake."

"No mistake."

He scowled but complied.

JD slapped the cuffs around his wrists, and Faulkner and Erickson escorted him down the walkway to the patrol car. Paul hobbled along, still stunned.

I read him his rights. "You have the right to remain silent..."

We interviewed him after he was processed and printed. The *sexual battery* charge would be a slam dunk once we had acquired his DNA. The murder charge might prove a little more difficult. It would be best to extract a confession.

Paul sat in the interrogation room with a tense look on his face.

JD and I took a seat across the table from him. I shook my head in utter dismay. "I just don't understand how a person could do such a thing. Please explain it to me. You know, on second thought, I don't think I want to know what you were thinking."

Paul said nothing.

"I've got a court order that says I can take a sample of your DNA. So there's no sense in arguing."

Worry tensed his face.

"You found out Skyler was pregnant. She was about to tell Deborah what you had been doing to her all those years. That would have destroyed you. You had to get rid of her. You figured you could blame it on the boyfriend or the guy she was having an affair with or a random serial killer. You either bought the barrel from Randy Murdock, or you stole it from the warehouse."

Paul remained silent.

"It doesn't really matter if you confess or not," I said, hoping for a little reverse psychology. "A first-degree felony sexual battery charge against a minor will be enough to put you away for the rest of your life. Might as well admit to the murder."

"I want to speak with an attorney."

"Sure thing. But an attorney isn't gonna help you." I opened the DNA collection kit, snapped on nitrile gloves, and pulled out the swab. "We can do this the easy way or the hard way. But I will get the sample."

Paul's face tensed.

He eventually complied, and we dropped the sample off at the lab. Paul was transferred to the housing pod. He'd be arraigned in the morning. The sexual battery charge was compounded by the fact he was a family member in custodial care. I wasn't sure if prosecutors would bring the murder charge just yet or wait until we had more evidence.

JD and I sat in the conference room, filling out after-action reports. There was no great sense of satisfaction. I was glad to have arrested Paul, but it didn't change the fact that something horrible had occurred all those years ago, and that uneasy feeling still lingered in the air.

I called Deborah and gave her the news.

She broke down into sobs. "Are you sure about this?"

"We'll have confirmation when the DNA comes back. But it's a foregone conclusion at this point. Do you remember anything odd about Paul's behavior the day of her disappearance?"

"He was worried at the time. At least, it appeared that way. I mistook his guilt and nervousness for concern." She was silent a moment, then suddenly gasped. "I remember he drove a pickup at the time. And now that I think about it, there was a steel drum in the back of his pickup that afternoon. It had been in the garage for a long time, and he said he was going to sell it to a friend who wanted to turn it into a barbecue pit. Oh, dear Lord! Please don't tell me Skyler was in that barrel."

I hated to tell her it was a distinct possibility. Paul had killed the girl in the afternoon when she came home from school. He stuffed her into the barrel and waited until he had a chance to dispose of it.

We chatted more, and I did my best to comfort her. Deborah agreed to testify against Paul should the need arise.

"Thank you for discovering the truth, as difficult as it is to hear," she said.

"You're welcome, Mrs. Locke. I wish things could have been different for Skyler."

"Me too, Deputy. Me too."

I ended the call and frowned.

"Don't take it so hard," JD said. "We got that scumbag."

"I know."

We wrapped up at the station and headed over to *Totally Tubular* to grab a bite to eat. It was a surf-themed bar with boards hanging from the ceiling and pictures of big waves.

Jack ordered coconut shrimp as an appetizer and a Tasty Tube Burger. I went with the mushroom cheeseburger.

In all the excitement of the morning, I had forgotten to call Crash and give him the bad news. I dialed his number. I figured he'd be out of bed by now, but there was never a guarantee with those guys. They were predominantly night owls.

Crash's scratchy voice filtered through the phone when he answered. "Yo, T! What's up?"

"Not much. Is Faye with you right now?"

"No, she just left."

"Did she tell you what happened with the band last night?" I asked gingerly.

"Yeah, I heard all about the drama."

"And you're cool with everything?" I asked, just to make sure he'd been given the full story.

"Yeah. I'm not thrilled about it. But we were split up at the time. What am I gonna do? She was honest with me about it."

"Okay, cool. Just FYI, *Lip Bomb* needs a bass player now."

He laughed. "Count me out. I'd never hear the end of it if I filled in for her."

I chuckled. "I understand. I'll catch you later."

I breathed a sigh of relief after ending the call. "Well, that went easier than expected."

"He's at the point where there's nothing to deter him," JD said. He shook his head. "Faye sure does like to start drama, doesn't she?"

"She has a gift for it."

We finished up and headed back to the car. We were walking down the sidewalk when Denise called. "Guess who just got arrested for shoplifting."

"I have no idea."

"Jared's brother, Trevor Landis. Trevor and a buddy skipped school and tried to five-finger a Rolex from the boutique at the Highland Village Mall. He wants to talk to you. Asked for you by name."

"Really? We'll be right there."

I told JD, and we climbed into the Porsche and zipped back to the station.

40

"I can give you what you want," Trevor said, handcuffed in the interrogation room.

"Start talking," I said.

"Not until we have a deal." Trevor was a sharp kid.

"What kind of deal do you want?" I knew exactly what he wanted.

"I get my little brother to tell you who paid him to swap the license plates on April's car, and my legal problems go away." He flashed a bright smile.

"What makes you think I'll take that deal?"

"I figure you'll do whatever it takes to find out who killed your cop buddy."

"How do you know your little brother is going to cooperate?"

"Because I'll beat his ass if he doesn't."

I looked at JD. He was all for it.

"Let me take it to the powers that be. I'm sure we can come to an agreement."

He flashed a confident smile. "I know that we can."

A guard buzzed us out of the interrogation room, and I called Todd McLean, an assistant district attorney, and pitched the deal. We had worked on a few cases previously, and I knew he'd go for it. It was a no-brainer. It didn't take long to have an agreement drafted. Trevor signed on the dotted line. If his little brother gave us information that led to the arrest and conviction of Chuck's killers, Trevor would walk—a fair enough trade.

I called Trevor's mother and informed her of the situation. She brought Jared up to the station as soon as he got out of school. I escorted them into the conference room and offered them a seat.

JD and I sat across the table from them, and Sheriff Daniels stood in the corner.

Jared remained tightlipped and surveyed us with suspicious eyes.

"Go ahead, Jared," his mother said. "Tell these gentlemen what they want to know."

"What's in it for me?"

"You get your brother out of jail."

"I will repeat the question. What's in it for me?"

His mother's face tensed. "You get to make it to your 13th birthday. That's what's in it for you."

"I want his room."

She scowled at him.

"I want his room or no deal."

"Don't push me, Jared."

"You gotta give to get."

The kid drove a hard bargain. I had to give him that.

"You're about to cross a line," his mother threatened.

Jared stood firm, folding his arms. He said nothing.

His mother finally caved. "Fine. You can have his room."

Jared smiled, "Ain't nobody gonna know I said something, right?"

"There may be a point in time where you may be required to testify," I said.

Concern bathed his mother's face. "Meaning everyone would know that my son was the rat? What if these people decide to retaliate?"

"We can provide protective services, and we can discuss the witness security program," I said.

"You mean, go into hiding? Uproot our whole lives?"

"Trevor is charged with felony theft," Daniels reminded her. "He just had a birthday yesterday, I believe. That makes him an adult. This is the kind of thing that sticks with you for the rest of your life."

It was a convincing argument. Mrs. Landis wasn't thrilled about the situation. "Go ahead, Jared. Tell them."

She glared at us.

"I was riding my bike through the neighborhood. These two dudes rolled up and asked if I wanted to make $50 bucks. I told those creeps to get lost. Random dude offers a kid $50 bucks, he wants his dick sucked."

"Jared!"

"It's true! But the dude was like, *no man, it ain't like that. All you gotta do is swap these plates out.* He pointed to April's car and gave me the plates. I rode my bike down the street, swapped them out, and gave them April's. He gave me $50 bucks."

"What kind of car were they driving?"

"It was a maroon Yamota with a matte black hood and a bunch of dents. The car was a piece of junk."

"You get a license plate?"

He smiled. "I sure did. I got a photographic memory. I'm gifted."

"If only you'd apply yourself," his mother chided.

Jared told me the plate number. I asked him to stay put while we looked up the information.

The vehicle belonged to Kashton Epps.

I kicked myself for not pursuing the lead sooner when Denise first mentioned him.

Kashton was no stranger to the inside of a prison. He was 24, with prior charges for drug possession, stolen property, and resisting arrest. Chuck had been the arresting officer on the possession charge, catching him with 2 kilos of cocaine. He shouldn't have been back on the street.

Kashton's face was crinkled with a guilty smirk in his mugshot. He had short brown hair that was receding at the temples. He had a thin brown beard and brown eyes.

His co-defendant in the possession charge was a guy named Isaac Norwood. They had both gotten off with a fine. Norwood was 23 with a similar background of possession charges, petty theft, and a DUI. He tilted his head back in his mugshot, trying to look like a badass. He had a look on his face as if to say, "This don't mean nothing to me."

Norwood had buzzed reddish-brown hair, a thick neck, and beefy shoulders. He had light eyes and puffy cheeks.

I printed their mugshots and took the images back to the conference room. "Do these two guys look familiar?"

Jared studied the images carefully. "Yeah. That's them."

"You're sure?"

"No doubt about it."

41

"Coconut County!" I shouted. "We have a warrant."

Before I could finish the words, Erickson and Faulkner heaved a battering ram against the door. The jam splintered, and the door flung open. Shards of wood scattered, and the inside door handle clanked against the foyer wall, denting the drywall.

JD tossed in two flash-bang grenades. They bounced across the tile, down the foyer, and clattered into the living room.

Bam!

Bam!

The deafening blasts rattled windows, and flashes like lightning blinded the room.

I stormed in with my weapon drawn, advancing down the foyer to the living room.

The two perps sat on the couch.

Isaac Norwood reached for an Uzi on the coffee table. It rested amid an array of empty beer bottles and a kilo of cocaine. He had been cutting it with laxative and packaging it into smaller units. A nearby tray contained marijuana, and there was an ashtray full of cigarette butts. The place smelled like a mix of the above substances combined with the acrid smell of the flash-bang grenades.

A thin haze hung in the air.

The perps lived in the *Windswept Dunes* apartments—a trashy little complex on the northeast side of Coconut Key. There were no dunes, and *Wind Damaged* might have been a more appropriate name.

Kashton held a video game controller in his hands as he raised them in the air. He'd been playing a first-person shooter on a 65-inch flatscreen display in the living room. The sound filtered from massive speakers.

The thugs had a lot of nice toys in the crappy apartment. Two fully tricked-out mountain bikes, a Les Paul guitar with a flame maple top and a small practice amp, nice furniture —all paid for with cash, no doubt.

Isaac's hand was almost an inch away from the submachine gun when he had a change of heart. Barrels of assault rifles in your face, wielded by angry cops, can have that effect. Isaac leaned away slowly and raised his hands in the air.

Within moments, we had the suspects face down on the ground, their hands cuffed behind their backs.

Erickson and Faulkner escorted them out of the apartment and down the steps to a patrol car waiting on the street.

We searched the apartment and confiscated drugs, machine guns, and fat stacks of cash. There was no doubt in my mind the ballistics from the machine guns would match the bullets that killed Chuck.

The scumbags were taken to the station, processed, and printed. They were lucky to still be breathing. Cop killers don't get a lot of leniency.

Between the two of them, I figured Kashton would be the first one to break. He looked like the softer of the two. There was more fear in his eyes. He was thin and twitchy. Isaac was a cool customer. Nothing seemed to phase him. He was disconnected emotionally.

We let them sit for a long time before entering the interrogation room. JD and I took a seat across from Kashton.

I sat there with a confident look on my face and stared at the perp for a long moment. "Okay. Here's the deal. Isaac said you were the shooter."

Kashton's eyes rounded, and his face tensed.

"He admitted to driving the vehicle," I said. "He's gonna get a considerably lesser sentence."

I was making the whole thing up.

Kashton's nervous eyes flicked about, and his cheeks reddened. I knew I had him. "That's bullshit. He is lying. I drove. He shot."

"That's not what he says. Why should I believe you over him?"

"Because that's the way it went down!!"

"Tell me why it went down in the first place. A vendetta against Deputy Atwood for your previous arrest?"

"Man, we were just doing what we were told."

I exchanged a curious glance with JD.

"So, who told you to kill Chuck Atwood?"

42

W hat Kashton said didn't surprise me.

But it did fill me with rage. My stomach twisted, and my hands balled into fists when he said that Stella Turner had ordered the hit on Chuck Atwood.

Normally, I wouldn't give much merit to an outlandish claim by a hoodlum. But this wasn't a normal situation.

"You're sure about that?" I asked.

"Positive. She said that Deputy Atwood was starting to cause problems for her."

I didn't need to ask what kind of problems. Chuck had gotten suspicious about Stella's Fund just like we had. Maybe he had damning evidence against the state attorney. Maybe he threatened to expose her. All kinds of scenarios entered my mind. I hated to think it. But what if Chuck had been blackmailing her?

"This all sounds good," I said. "But nobody's gonna believe you. You're not credible."

"Yeah, they are. I got proof!"

"What kind of proof?"

"Let's talk a deal first."

"Everybody wants a deal," I said in a resigned tone. "Tell me what you got."

"No. I walk away from this, or you don't get the audio."

"Audio?"

"I recorded our conversations with Turner. I'm not stupid. Isaac is the stupid one."

That was debatable. They were both pretty dumb if you asked me.

"Let's hear the audio. Where is it?"

"It's on my phone. I'll play it for you. But you drop the charges against me first."

"What about your buddy?"

"Fuck him. He ratted me out."

I loved it when perps turned against each other.

"Hang tight a minute," I said.

I left the interrogation room, retrieved his personal belongings, and brought the phone back. It was a brand-new phone with facial recognition. All I had to do was hold it in front of his face.

The security screen vanished, and I started scrolling through the device, looking in the voice recording app. I clicked a file labeled Stella Turner. It wasn't the highest quality audio in the world. There was a lot of mic noise and rustling as Kashton surreptitiously recorded the conversation.

The woman's voice was unmistakable. It was Stella Turner.

There was a lot of dead space and small talk back and forth between Isaac and Kashton as they waited for Stella to arrive. It sounded like a car pulled up, and the two thugs opened the door and climbed inside. The door slammed with a clunk.

"You said you needed to talk in person," Isaac said.

"I've got a job for you," Stella said. "You do this and your problems go away for a long time. Whenever you get in trouble, I'll make sure it gets taken care of."

"I'd like a little more intel, so we don't get in trouble in the first place."

"You pull this off smoothly, you boys will be able to grow your operation. I guarantee it."

"What do we have to do?"

"Deputy Atwood needs an early retirement."

"You want us to kill a cop?"

"Is that a problem for you?"

There was a long silence.

"No," Isaac said.

"You ever done anything like that before?"

"You're honestly asking me to admit a crime to a state attorney?"

Stella laughed. "You're smarter than you look."

"When do you want it done?"

"As soon as possible. It needs to look like gang-related violence. A traffic stop gone bad. Something like that."

"We can do that," Isaac said. "Why do you want him dead?"

"Don't tell me you need a reason to kill a cop?"

"Just curiosity."

"He's a danger to me. And what's dangerous to me is dangerous to you. He knows too much, and he's asking questions."

It was all I needed to hear. "Where was this audio captured?"

"In her car."

I texted the recording to my device, then pushed away from the table and started toward the door.

"Hey, what about my deal?"

I ignored him and pushed into the hallway. Daniels joined us, having watched from the observation room. His face was tense with anger, his cheeks flush. "I'll get a warrant."

"She's doing something illegal with the Forward Fund, and Atwood found out about it," I said.

"I want her in jail by the end of the day. Do this by the book, no screw-ups. This is going to raise a lot of hell."

43

It was a spectacle—Stella Turner, surrounded by pissed-off deputies on the courthouse steps —priceless.

"Stella Turner, you're under arrest for conspiracy to commit murder," I said with glee.

A look of utter shock and disbelief twisted on her face. "This is outrageous!"

"Yes. It is."

JD slapped the cuffs around her wrists, and Faulkner took her by the arm. He ushered her down the steps toward the patrol car as people gawked. I may have tipped off Paris Delaney. She was there with her crew, filming the whole thing.

Stella knew enough to keep her mouth shut. She wouldn't talk, but it was fun to watch her squirm in the interrogation room. We had damning evidence, and I felt certain Stella

Turner was going to go away for a long time, and I told her as much.

After we filled out after-action reports, JD and I headed over to *Wetsuit* for a celebratory cocktail and dinner. He lifted his glass of whiskey to toast. "One by one, we're gonna clean up this town."

I laughed. It was a tall order.

After dinner, we headed to the practice studio. Crash had gotten his cast off. It was his first day back with the band. They ran through their setlist, and Crash was a little rusty on the first song but snapped back into the groove quickly. He was still weak and sore, and he iced his wrist afterward. But he was on the road to a full recovery. Hopefully, things would be getting back to normal.

Faye attended practice and cheered Crash on. It seemed like they had gotten through their rough patch and were moving forward.

As usual, we hit *Tide Pool* afterward and returned to the *Avventura* for a late-night gathering. There was an awkward moment of tension when Sadie joined us, but the girls stayed amicable. Sadie wasn't looking to have her back in the band anytime soon, but they were at least on speaking terms.

"She didn't sleep with *my* boyfriend," Sadie said to me. "I got no real beef with her. I'm just mad about how it all went down."

Sadie did her best to convince me to sit in with *Lip Bomb*. She made a good persuasive argument, and I was happy to let her give it her best shot.

A call first thing in the morning woke me up. I wiped the sleep from my eyes and grabbed the phone from the nightstand. The sheriff's annoyed voice filtered through the speaker. "You're not gonna believe this shit."

"What happened?"

"The charges against Stella Turner were dropped."

"What!?"

"The audio recording was deemed inadmissible. Florida is a consent state. All parties must consent to the recording. Stella obviously didn't, and since the conversation took place in her car, she had a reasonable expectation of privacy."

I groaned. "Who was the judge?"

"Echols."

"Figures."

"Turn on the news. It's a media frenzy. Word is she's going to resign but it looks like she's gonna walk away from this without any time."

"Not if I can help it."

"That's what I was hoping you'd say. Find something and make it stick."

"I will."

I turned on the TV. There were images of Stella leaving the courthouse, mobbed by reporters. Cameras flashed, and microphones were shoved in her face. She had no comment as she pushed through the crowd.

I texted the audio file to Paris Delaney. What the hell... It may not have been admissible in court, but the court of public opinion had less rigid standards.

Paris texted back. *[Now that's what I call juicy. I owe you one.]*

[It didn't come from me.]

[You know I protect my sources.]

That much was true. She'd go to her grave with her sources.

Within minutes, the audio was a breaking news alert. Soon, it was all over the Internet. Stella Turner was finished professionally. At least, that's what I hoped. But she'd probably get a book deal and make millions.

Isabella called after breakfast. "I see your friend is making headlines."

"She is not my friend."

"I did some digging."

"Tell me something good."

44

"Stella is on the board of the Forward Fund," Isabella said. "They paid out over $3 million to various nonprofits that didn't even apply for grants. All of those companies paid a consulting fee to Sunbeam Analytics. That company is owned by an offshore company named Sunray Strategies, of which I am still trying to ascertain the ownership. But I will bet you Stella Turner has a hand in that."

"She's funneling money into the fund, giving it out to her friends who are then paying her consulting fees," I said.

"It appears that way."

"Is that illegal?"

"It's unethical, that's for sure. The legality depends on what you'll be able to prove and how the deals were structured. Plus, you're not gonna be able to use anything I provide you with. You'll have to pull all this information on your own. My suspicion is this has been going on for years, and nobody wants to do anything about it."

"You got that right. Too many people are getting rich, and no prosecuting attorney wants to open that can of worms."

"There are two things you can do. Sunbeam Analytics has made numerous political contributions to local office holders. I'd scrutinize those transactions. You might be able to catch her on an election law violation. Also, I checked her personal financial records. She just purchased a new car from Hartsell imports at a substantial discount. I think this is where she screwed up. If that discount was given in exchange for some type of deferred prosecution agreement, that is a direct violation."

I grinned. "You're brilliant."

"Yes, I am."

I thanked Isabella and ended the call.

I climbed out of bed, showered, dressed, then shuffled down the steps and banged on the hatch to JD's stateroom. "Get your ass up. We've got work to do. Stella got off."

I knew that would get his attention.

I went into the galley and started cooking breakfast. Afterward, we headed across the island to *Hartsell Imports*. The lot was loaded with slightly used luxury and exotic cars. There were Lamborghinis, Ferraris, Porches, Jaguars, Bentleys, Aston Martins. All polished and shiny, their tires slick with protectant.

We stepped into the showroom, and that new car smell filled the air, even though the cars weren't exactly new. They were all low mileage. Cars that wealthy collectors bought that sat in driveways and saw little use.

A slick salesman approached. "What can I do for you, gentlemen?"

"Looking for Nick Hartsell?"

"May I tell him your name?"

I flashed my badge. "Deputy Tyson Wild."

He forced a smile. "Give me one minute. I'll let him know you're here."

He spun around and marched to the back office.

Nick Hartsell emerged a few moments later. He had short wavy blond hair, a tanned face, and a square jaw. He wore a white linen suit and a royal blue dress shirt. He looked like a TV star, and I recognized him from his commercials. The 47-year-old had blue eyes and a bright smile. A thin gold chain hung around his neck. He was a wheeler-dealer and could get just about any car you wanted for a price. He extended a welcoming hand. "Deputies, welcome to Hartsell Imports."

We shook.

"Is there something I can interest you in? We offer law enforcement discounts."

"Actually, that's what I'm here to talk to you about."

"You came to the right place." He sized me up quickly. "You look like a Lambo guy. I've got a Huracán EVO Spyder in neon green with your name on it. 3,200 miles. Almost new."

"Tempting, but I'd like to talk to you about another deal you made. You recently sold Stella Turner a convertible Jaguar."

He hesitated. "I sell a lot of people a lot of cars."

"According to my records, you took a loss on the vehicle."

"And what records are those?"

"I can't disclose my sources."

He shrugged. "You win some, you lose some," he said, growing uncomfortable.

"You strike me as the kind of guy that doesn't like to lose money on deals."

His face tensed. "Perhaps we should have this conversation in my office."

He led us down a hallway and ushered us into his office. He shut the door and offered us a seat. It was an elegant space. Sleek and minimal. There were pictures on the walls of Nick with various celebrity clients and expensive cars. The furniture was stylish, and the office was tidy. There was a large flatscreen display on his desk and a keyboard.

He took a seat behind his desk.

"I'll cut to the chase," I said. "I know you received favorable treatment from Stella in the past. In case you haven't been watching the news, those days are over."

He tried not to frown.

"In light of your son's current legal problems, I think you might want to cooperate with me."

"What are you offering?"

"The car you sold Stella... that was part of your agreement to make your son's legal problems go away. I need you to testify to that fact—full immunity, of course."

"I deal with a lot of clients that require discretion. Some of them will be leery of doing business with me if I become a prosecutor witness."

"Your boy is facing another DUI and reckless driving charge, among other things."

"At the rate he's crashing my cars, maybe I should leave him in jail."

I chuckled.

"I help you put away Stella Turner on corruption charges, and Cameron's DUI goes away?"

As much as I hated to see that little punk get off, I wanted to see Stella behind bars more. "It would appear that way."

"And you've talked to one of the assistant district attorneys about this deal?"

"I have," I said, though I hadn't yet talked to Todd McLean.

Nick thought about it for a moment.

45

"Okay," Nick said, nodding his head. "I sold her the car. I took a $20K hit on it. She said if I did that and contributed another $20K to her *fund*," he said in air quotes, "Cameron's latest indiscretion would disappear."

"Would you be willing to come down to the station now and make a formal statement?" I asked.

"If it gets Cameron's latest charge resolved, sure. Let's do it. But keep my name out of the papers."

"I'll try."

I made a few phone calls. McLean signed off on the deal. Nick made his statement, and we got another warrant. This time we arrested Stella at her home.

Again, she said nothing.

She was arraigned the next morning and made bail. She put up the million dollars and was back on the street.

It was depressing to see. But I had to keep faith in the system.

We kept digging into the Forward Fund and the transactions the organization made. Ellie agreed to let us search Chuck's laptop, and we found a goldmine of information. He'd done his homework and had found numerous suspicious transfers, donations, and consulting agreements. He was on the verge of exposing everything.

Paris started an ongoing investigation series. And I alerted the Florida Election Commission.

Stella was on her way down—for good this time.

I saw on the news where Randy Murdoch had died from a heart attack. The stress must have been too much for him. There was no doubt in my mind he'd had an inappropriate relationship with Skyler. But that was moot now.

I felt bad for his wife.

JD and I took a couple days off to relax. We fished, drank, searched for treasure, and chased skirts. So, it really wasn't any different from normal.

Faye reached out to Katie and tried to mend fences. She blamed her actions on too much alcohol and poor choices. It didn't really change things between them, but at least she made the effort.

Crash agreed to sit in with *Lip Bomb* for one show. In the meantime, he gave me lessons, and I practiced as much as possible. I was having fun with it. The guys let me jam a few songs with them at practices.

Things were going good. Summer was almost upon us. Crime was at a minimum. No assassins showed up in the night to kill me. It almost seemed normal.

That would end soon.

We made our plans to attend the red carpet premiere of *Bree* in LA. The studio flew us out on a private jet, and JD got a chance to reconnect with his daughter. He hadn't seen Scarlett in a while.

The limo driver picked us up from the FBO at Burbank, drove over the hill, and headed down Highland. We turned onto Sunset, traveling west, then winded our way up to a nice home in the Hollywood Hills. The driver pulled into the circular drive, hopped out, and grabbed our doors. He pulled our luggage from the trunk as we walked to the front door and rang the bell.

An excited Scarlett answered with a shriek. She bounced up and down and gave us both hugs. JD held on for a long time. The Skyler Locke case had struck a chord with him, as it would with any parent. He was lucky to have her in his life, and he was going to soak up every minute with her. His eyes grew a little misty.

"I'm so glad you guys are here!" Scarlett said. "Let me show you around."

She ushered us into the foyer, and I tipped the limo driver after he brought the bags inside.

"So this is what you wanted to show us," Jack said, looking around in awe.

"I wanted it to be a surprise."

With Scarlett's newfound success, she had purchased a home in the hills. It wasn't the biggest house in Hollywood, but it was sleek and modern with a pool and a stunning view that looked over the hills and Century City.

"What do you think?"

JD was impressed. "Can you afford this?"

She looked at him flatly. "I can right now." She crossed her fingers. "Hopefully, Ultra Mega 2 does well. Ultra Mega 3 is when the real money will come in." She smiled.

"Just don't get yourself overleveraged."

"I won't. I've worked hard. I'm entitled to a little splurge."

"This is more than a little splurge."

She scowled at him. "Stop being such a party pooper. You are in no position to lecture on excess."

She had a point.

Scarlett showed us to the guest rooms, and we got settled in.

We went to a fancy restaurant in the hills and attended a few industry parties. Scarlett spent most of the next day getting dolled up by a professional make-up artist and stylist for the premiere. Fabian Fabron, a top designer, loaned her a $95K dress. She'd be photographed and filmed by every news outlet on the red carpet. It was free advertising.

When the time arrived, the limousine drove us down to the famous Chinese Theater. Cameras flashed, and the crowd cheered as we stepped out of the limousine into the limelight. Scarlett smiled and waved to her adoring fans.

We followed behind her, nobody caring who we were.

She stopped at every interview station along the way, talking about the film, the upcoming *Ultra Mega 2*, and what was next for the young starlet. With her hair coiffed to perfection, dressed in a sparkling gown and brilliant diamonds around her neck, on loan from a boutique on Rodeo, she looked like Hollywood royalty. After tonight, she'd be on the cover of every magazine.

We mixed and mingled with all the Hollywood types. My agent, Joel, greeted us with a smile and a hug. He was dressed in a stylish navy suit with a matching pocket square. His blond hair was buzzed short on the sides and spiked on top. "This is a big night. Are you ready?"

"It's taken a long time to get here," I said.

"The buzz is good," he whispered. "Trust me, there are great things ahead."

Usually, the words *trust me* were followed by lies. But Joel was the rare exception in Hollywood.

We bumped into Susan, the head of the studio, and chatted for a minute about upcoming projects. She was still on me to set up an office on the studio lot and develop more projects. She was out of her mind if she thought I'd leave Coconut Key. Despite everything, it was home.

We finally took our seats. The lights went down, and the picture came up on the big screen. The studio's logo flashed, and the movie started at the moment when I first met Bree —on the plane to France.

It was surreal. Like a memory, but not.

Scarlett looked fantastic on screen with her shoulder-length blonde hair and sparkling eyes. She captured Bree's essence. But more than that, her own spark shined through.

My phone buzzed my pocket. I pulled it out discreetly and looked at the screen. A text from Sheriff Daniels read: *[I need you boys back in Coconut Key ASAP. We've got another dead body.]*

Ready for more?
The adventure continues with Wild Envy!

Join my newsletter and find out what happens next!

AUTHOR'S NOTE

Thanks for all the great reviews!

I've got more adventures for Tyson and JD. Stay tuned.

If you liked this book, let me know with a review on Amazon.

Hope you are well during this challenging time. Thanks for reading!

—*Tripp*

TYSON WILD

Wild Ocean

Wild Justice

Wild Rivera

Wild Tide

Wild Rain

Wild Captive

Wild Killer

Wild Honor

Wild Gold

Wild Case

Wild Crown

Wild Break

Wild Fury

Wild Surge

Wild Impact

Wild L.A.

Wild High

Wild Abyss

Wild Life

Wild Spirit

Wild Thunder

Wild Season

Wild Rage

Wild Heart

Wild Spring

Wild Outlaw

Wild Revenge

Wild Secret

Wild Envy

Wild...

CONNECT WITH ME

I'm just a geek who loves to write. Follow me on Facebook.

www.trippellis.com

Made in the USA
Monee, IL
24 August 2021

76442906R00146